Under Starry Skies

ANITA K. GREENE

Anita K. Greene

UNDER STARRY SKIES
An Original Work by Anita K. Greene

Published by Cedar Lake Studio

ISBN 978-0-9886709-5-2

Cover Design by Wicked Smart Designs
Interior Formatting by Author E.M.S.

Published in the United States of America.

To my wonderful sisters

Janice, my oldest sibling and oldest sister,
and
Candace, my youngest sibling and youngest sister.
Without you, I wouldn't be who I am ~
The middle sister!

There are no perfect words to express
how much I love each of you.

I'm so thankful that God had us born
into the same family.

Hugs and kisses!

Under Starry Skies

SeaMount Series Book Three

SeaMount diver, Ethan Thomas is surveying the floor of a shipping canal when a woman's face appears wavering ethereal as sea smoke in the swaying weeds. The vision cracks open the sealed chambers of his heart. Can he move beyond the grief that has held him captive?

Talia Combs has her life all figured out. A career she enjoys, a home she loves, and the best in Alzheimer's nursing care for Papa. But then Agent Thomas steps into her life, and everything she thought she knew about herself and her family is turned upside down. Can Talia forgive her Papa for the secrets he kept?

Together, will they trust God even when they do not understand where He is leading them?

He heals the brokenhearted
and binds up their wounds.
He determines the number of the stars
and calls them each by name.
Great is our Lord and mighty in power;
his understanding has no limit.

Psalm 147:3-5

Under Starry Skies

Chapter 1

A kitchen stove, wicker chair, and computer monitor lay eerily out of place in the murky underwater world. With his tactical suit protecting him from the brackish canal water, Ethan Thomas swam deeper. Whit McCord kept pace at his side. To their left, the St. John twins made up a second swim pair.

A week ago the earth had quaked, and a tsunami had rolled over the coastal towns of this small country perched on the edge of the Pacific Rim. The Prime Minister had asked the SeaMount team to help with the disaster clean up.

Outfitted with rebreathers, the men worked in silence surveying the floor of the canal. Clearing the waterway would allow supplies to be shipped inland to thousands of displaced survivors.

A box truck leaned against a ledge of volcanic rock, its back bumper buried in mud. The tumble into the canal had disintegrated its windows. With short fin strokes, Ethan approached. The cab sat high in the water creating a hazard. If he found human remains, he'd flag it with a buoy for the recovery team.

Peering inside from every angle, he didn't see any indication a driver had been at the wheel. He attached a small, inexpensive transponder to the truck and signaled an "all clear" to McCord. With a flick of his fins, he turned away. Mid stroke, his heart slammed against the wall of his chest.

On the floor of the canal a dark feminine face wavered ethereal as sea smoke in the undulating vegetation.

Heart thudding, he blinked hard to clear his vision. His nerves pinged from the top of his hooded head to his toes encased in booties and fins. He scanned the swaying weeds again. *There.* Her luminous eyes held him transfixed.

A hand squeezed his shoulder. Ethan swung around coming face mask to mask with McCord.

McCord signed, "OK?"

The sea grass swept about her face like glossy strands of hair. Ethan pointed at her.

McCord looked in the direction Ethan indicated and shook his head, questioning.

Ethan gestured again, desperate for his swim buddy to catch sight of her. *Lord, who is she?* The prayer shot to the surface of his scrambled thoughts.

The St. John brothers glided closer.

McCord shook his open hand signaling there was a problem and motioned for the men to surface.

Ethan wanted to refuse, but he was one against three combat swimmers-turned-mother-hens. As big as he was, he wouldn't win. McCord and the brothers pressed close on all sides. He glanced over his shoulder. *What was God showing him?* Though he was familiar with revelations in his dreams, this vision had materialized before his open eyes.

He broke through the choppy surface of the windswept canal.

Caleb Fallon stood at the helm of the flat bottom boat the host country had loaned the team. The shallow draft made the boat perfect for their work. The propeller remained motionless allowing the divers to safely approach.

Grabbing a handgrip, Ethan pulled himself over the gunnel taking care not to damage the rebreather strapped to his chest. He removed his mouthpiece and mask. At his side, McCord went through the same motions.

"What was that all about?" Whit's green gaze tracked the length of Ethan, looking for a problem.

Ethan sucked in air, deep and fast. "I saw…." He gulped. All the men were listening. "I saw a woman."

McCord pulled back. Uncertainty swept across his features. "A body?"

"No." Ethan slipped off his hood. "Just her face."

Wary, the other agents watched him. What he'd accepted long ago as a gift from God, messed with the heads of everyone around him.

Whit glanced at the others before nailing Ethan with a piercing look. "Tell us *exactly* what you saw."

His thoughts careened, wild and chaotic. "A woman's face." Framed by the light sable of her skin, her eyes had sparkled like stars.

"Who is she?"

Caleb's SAT phone beeped. He stepped away to quietly answer it.

"Don't know." Ethan peeled off his gloves and watched the sunlight glint in the droplets of water dotting his mahogany skin. The sight of the woman reverberated in the deepest chambers of his soul. Chambers he'd sealed two years ago when he buried his wife and young son on the same day.

"For you." Caleb shoved the SAT phone at him. "The director."

What did Sam Traven want? "Hello."

"We've found a woman who is related to Simao and Angelina."

Ethan's breath stalled in his chest. Three months earlier, a SeaMount agent had rescued two orphans from the war-torn island of St. Beatrice. Since that time the director had been trying to find a living family member.

Sam's gravelly voice grated in Ethan's ear. "An aunt lives in New York City."

Ethan exhaled in a whistling *swoosh*. Certainty settled over him. *The woman in his vision.*

Chapter 2

Talia Combs discreetly pressed the security button hidden beneath the edge of her desk. "Carlos, please put down the knife. We can work this out." She was tall, but this young man stood a head taller.

"No." Carlos slashed the air between them. "There's *nothin'* to work out."

Talia fought the panic rising in her chest. The last bell of the day had rung, and he'd lingered behind as the other students left. "There are always options, Carlos."

As a music teacher in a school for children with psychiatric and behavioral needs, she had faced a great deal in her classroom, but never a knife. How had he gotten it through security protocols? Realizing he'd carried it all day, she shuddered. She didn't know what he hoped to accomplish by pulling it out now. A volatile teen, perhaps he didn't know either.

"You don't understand." He mussed his jet-black hair with a sweep of his hand.

"Try me." *Keep him talking.* Grasping the edge of the desk, she pressed the button again.

"What do *you* know? Bet you never watched your mother get dragged away by the cops."

"You're right." Talia's mother had died when she was

very young. She didn't remember the woman who'd birthed her. "But taking your anger out on me won't change what happened." In her peripheral vision she saw a flicker of movement at the classroom door. Keeping her eyes trained on Carlos, she continued to talk. "Let's sit and put our heads together. Perhaps Mr. Dunn in guidance can help us find out where the authorities took your little brother."

A dark form loomed behind Carlos. In rapid succession the teen was disarmed and anchored in a neck hold that demanded compliance.

Knees too weak to support her any longer, Talia dropped into her chair. "Thank you, God."

A giant of a man stood behind Carlos. His smile flashed brilliant against his dark skin. "Amen to that."

Mr. Finnegan, the school's dean, hurried through the doorway. Two security officers followed. From the safety of her chair, Talia watched them secure Carlos and lead him away.

The dean shook the big man's hand, thanking him. "We're fortunate you came by." He shifted to face Talia. "Oddly enough he's here to see you."

"Me?" She straightened in her chair. "We've never met."

An easy smile bent his lips. "Let me correct the oversight." He held out his hand. "How do you do. I'm Ethan Thomas." A drawl edged the musical lilt of his voice.

Functioning on autopilot Talia extended her hand. His warm grasp swallowed it up.

Mr. Finnegan dragged two chairs to the front of her desk. "Please sit, Mr. Thomas." Not waiting for his guest to be seated first, Mr. Finnegan dropped into his chair. He pulled out his handkerchief and wiped his brow. "I'll have to review tapes and see how Carlos got that knife through security." He tucked his handkerchief away. "When such an incident happens," he swiveled toward his guest, "not that this happens often. We're proud of our good record. But," he turned back to Talia, "when something this alarming *does* happen, the teacher is encouraged to take some time off."

Talia shook her head. "I'm fine." She clasped her hands together hoping to stop the trembling. "Really, I'm fine."

Mr. Finnegan held up his hand. "You'll miss the three weeks before Christmas break. You can return when school starts again after the New Year." His voice softened. "You'll need the time and not just because of what happened here. Mr. Thomas has some information to share with you."

Talia ignored most of what the dean said. "What information?" Her gaze bounced between the two men, before settling on Ethan Thomas.

He balanced precariously on a student chair too small for his large frame. "I'm here about your family."

Panic plucked at the nerves in Talia's solar plexus. She swept her fingers across her brow, gold bracelets jangling. "My father? The nursing facility is rated one of the best."

Ethan Thomas shook his head. "I'm here about Maria Rivas, your sister."

Confusion rippled through Talia. "I don't have a sister." *Was that regret shadowing his brown eyes?* "Who are you exactly?"

He pulled out his wallet and placed a crisp white business card in front of her. "I work for the SeaMount Agency. Three months ago one of our agents was on the island of St. Beatrice."

Talia pressed her clenched hands against her stomach. St. Beatrice—her country of birth. She had been two years old when her father brought her to the United States.

"In the process of extracting an American citizen," he hesitated, "two children were removed from the island and taken to safety. Getting information about their family has taken time because of the civil war."

Talia had heard about the war on the news.

"The children are orphans. Their mother was your sister."

"You're wrong." She shook her head. "Why would my father bring me to the United States and leave my sister behind?"

"Your mother—"

"She died when I was a baby."

"Miss Combs, your mother passed away only five years ago."

Talia shot to her feet. Her chair rolled back and slammed against the wall. "I will *not* listen to your lies."

Both men rose.

She turned to Mr. Finnegan. "Please escort him out." Shaking, she grabbed her purse from the bottom drawer of her desk. Taking her winter coat and scarf from the wall hook, she bolted through the open door. "Oh." She stopped and hitched the strap of her purse higher on her shoulder. Both men remained standing in front of her desk. "I'll be here tomorrow as usual, Mr. Finnegan."

Chapter 3

Worship music filled the old theatre now serving as a church. A thousand voices lifted in sweet harmony soothing Ethan's soul. The day had proved difficult in more ways than he'd anticipated.

Witnessing Talia's face-off with a knife-wielding punk had almost stopped his heart. For one moment he thought he'd arrived too late. But she'd kept her cool, and he'd maneuvered into place before the kid knew what was happening. *Thank you, Lord.*

He had followed her from the school to her apartment, and then here. The midweek service offered her solace among fellow Christians. She had taken a seat three rows in front of him still unaware of his presence, attesting to her state of mind. Ordinarily his stature didn't allow him the luxury of getting lost in a crowd.

Her halo of flyaway curls stirred in the currents of heated air. Soft light glimmered in a tear on the curve of her cheek. Hands clasped together over her heart, she sang a few words before stopping to bite her lower lip. She struggled to regain control of her emotions before joining in on the chorus.

"Lord, she needs your peace." Ethan clenched his hand into a fist. "And Simao and Angelina need her."

The music ended. A rolling murmur of voices swelled

like a mighty wave as heartfelt praises and petitions were lifted en masse to the Throne of Grace. Whispering his own prayers, a flurry of movement captured Ethan's attention.

Talia had squeezed past fellow worshipers and was stepping into the aisle. Instead of going to the exit, she descended the stairs to the church's coffee shop.

Ethan followed at a discreet distance. With a congregation this large, people were constantly moving about in the building. He used that to his advantage. When she entered the coffee shop, he waited and watched from the hall's shadows. His vision of her in the murky canal water had been unerringly accurate with two exceptions—the real woman was more beautiful and more vibrant.

His assignment demanded he remain close to her, but he was honest enough with himself to recognize that more than duty kept his attention focused on her. He was drawn to Talia, and that attraction felt like a betrayal to his memories of Lacey. He loved his late wife, heart and soul. But his connection to her became more tenuous with each passing day, evaporating into the mists of time.

Seeing Talia carry her order to a table in the corner, Ethan entered the shop and ordered a black coffee. Sending a prayer winging heavenward, he approached her. "Good evening, Miss Combs."

Her startled expression grew cautious. "How did you find me?"

Ignoring the question, he eased into the chair opposite her. Tension hummed beneath the surface of his skin. "How are you doing?"

Her lips tightened into a straight line. "I'm fine."

He wouldn't argue the lie. She was speaking to him, which was more than he'd expected. "You were courageous today."

An involuntary sigh escaped her lips. Her shoulders relaxed just a little. "I kept talking, hoping and praying someone would come soon."

A shudder rippled through Ethan. Had he been delayed, or had Mr. Finnegan been in a meeting, the outcome could have been tragic.

"How old are the children?" Her words rasped soft between them.

Thank you, Lord. "Simao is nine, and Angelina, five." Working with the island's new regime, Sam had greased a few palms for information.

She broke off a piece of pastry and smashed it with her fingertip. "You're sure they're part of *my* family?"

Ethan pulled a photo from his pocket and slid it across the table.

Chapter 4

Two precious faces with a familiar family resemblance stared at Talia. Her fingers flew to her lips, and her breath caught in her throat.

"You don't remember your sister?" Ethan's soft voice was at odds with his demeanor and size.

"W-When I was small I asked my father about another child I vaguely remembered." Her heart pulsed hard. "He said she must have been a playmate." Bitterness burned through her as she recognized the lie by omission. She glared at the man across the table, not wanting to believe him. "Why didn't my father tell me I had a sister?"

He stared into his coffee. "Perhaps he didn't know *how* to tell you without causing heartache."

Talia shoved her plate away, bracelets clinking. "Well, whatever hurt he saved me from as a child, is doubly devastating now." She felt as though an invisible band was tightening around her chest making it hard to breathe.

"I'm sorry." In the low light of the coffee shop he fiddled with his mug.

He'd blown her life to bits, and all he had to offer was, "I'm sorry"? "So, what do you want from me?" Knowing she wasn't ready to hear that answer, she kept right on talking. "Where did you find them?"

"They lived on the streets, helped along by a man running a soup kitchen."

She gasped. "Lived on the streets? How…how did they survive?"

He hesitated.

"Be honest with me."

"Simao provided for himself and his sister by picking the pockets of tourists."

"Oh." She blinked, unable to hide her shock. "How long did they live like that?"

"A new regime is in power so we had to piece together the little the government gave us and what Simao has shared. After your sister passed away they lived with their grandmother—your mother. When she died, neighbors passed the children around, trying to care for them. The plan didn't hold together for long."

Talia picked up the photo and stared at the children. *What if they really were her niece and nephew?*

Her thoughts veered away. She loved her career as a teacher. Exploring the world of music with her students—the sounds, lyrics, and various instruments—was her passion. Her class was a safe place for creative expression. Many of her children came from tough situations. The time they spent in her class was not only fun, it also taught them new skills and helped prepare them for challenges they would face in the future.

She fingered the edge of the photo. What kind of future would Simao and Angelina have? Pain pierced her heart. *How could she help so many children but look away from family?*

The door of the elevator slid shut, and the floor numbers ticked down. Talia had been on her computer until the wee hours, searching for information about the SeaMount Agency. She read everything she found—which wasn't much. But there was enough to convince her that Ethan Thomas was not a nutcase. Good thing. She was accompanying him to Rhode Island. There she'd meet the children he said were her niece and nephew.

A bell dinged, and the door slid open. Her suitcase rolled off the elevator in her wake and rammed her heel. "Ouch."

"Let me take your luggage, Miss Combs." Ethan stepped forward.

Apprehension and anticipation swirled through Talia in a discordant symphony. She couldn't shake the feeling her life was about to change irrevocably. "Please call me Talia."

"Only if you address me as Ethan."

The smile that eased across his handsome, rough-hewn face did nothing to help settle the nerves in her stomach. His heavy winter jacket added bulk to his already large frame. Standing next to him she felt petite. Due to her height, it was a sensation she rarely felt in the presence of others.

"I called Mr. Finnegan." The dean's pleased response to her decision still rankled. She turned up the collar on her winter coat and pulled on fleece-lined gloves. "I have one stop to make before we leave the city."

Fingertips bouncing across the keypad, Talia entered the numerical code that released the electronic lock. Ethan reached around her and opened the door.

Morning light streamed through skylights brightening the neutral colors in the lounge and dining area. Private rooms encircled this hub of activity. High on one wall, a large screen television failed to hold captive the dozing audience. Over the muted voice of the news anchor drifted the melancholy notes of an alto saxophone.

Talia greeted a nurse helping an elderly woman with her orange juice. Circling to the left, she paused at a closed door and tapped before entering. "Good morning, Papa." Her heart wrenched. The first moment with him was always painful for her.

A shadow of his former self, he was seated on a straight back chair, the bow of the saxophone resting against his thigh. His fingers were stiff and his lungs weak. The immense repertoire of songs he'd once committed to memory had, one by one, slipped away. Only these six mournful notes remained.

Talia placed her hand on his shoulder. "Papa?"

He released the mouthpiece. "Hello."

She was a stranger standing before him. "Hello, Papa."

"I have a gig tonight."

"That's wonderful." Communicating with her father meant entering his world through whatever door he opened.

"I'm late for the bus." He tried to rise.

She pressed her hand to his shoulder. "No, Papa. The bus doesn't come for another hour." She blinked back tears. There was no gig, and there was no bus except in her father's confused mind. "I'm leaving for a few days, Papa." She pressed a kiss onto his tight gray curls. *What secrets did his mind hold captive?* Her heart ached as she rested her cheek on the top of his head and whispered, "Why didn't you tell me about my sister...and my mother?" She closed her eyes, steeling her resolve not to entertain the bitterness that was only a thought away. *Could she forgive him for keeping these secrets?*

Remembering Ethan's presence at the open doorway, she sniffed and straightened. "You take care, Papa. I love you." She kissed him once more. Blinded by a hot flow of tears, she spun away.

A strong hand pressed against the small of her back, and she leaned into its strength. At this moment, her independent spirit required some propping up. She let Ethan guide her toward the exit. Fingers trembling, she punched in the code to open the door. The sound of six sad notes followed her into the foyer and the world beyond lockdown.

Chapter 5

Descending the train car's metal steps, Ethan handed Talia's luggage to Charlie Watkins.

"Welcome home, Ethan." As SeaMount's resident geek and assistant to the director, Charlie kept the business side of SeaMount running smoothly. He was the only man at the Agency without military background.

"Thanks." Ethan helped Talia down. He'd given her his full attention on the train, but to his surprise, she barely spoke. Instead, she'd spent much of the time deep in thought…or prayer. He wasn't certain which. There was only one thing he was sure of—she would never hear the truth from her father.

In the gloom of late afternoon, a cold December wind sent a swirl of snowflakes across the parking lot of the historic train station. After helping Talia into the rear seat of the black SUV, Ethan climbed in beside her.

Charlie shifted the vehicle into gear and pulled out of the lot. "The team started hanging Christmas lights."

Ethan shook his head. "Thanksgiving was only last week."

"Like a bunch of kids itching for any excuse to party." Charlie glanced in the rearview mirror. "Aggie's up to her bun in flour. Insists there aren't enough days in December to finish the baking. The kids are on sugar highs."

Talia straightened and glanced at Ethan with a questioning look.

"Simao and Angelina celebrated Thanksgiving at SeaMount. Aggie moved into a suite with them for the time being."

A smile wisped across her lips before she faced the window to watch the brightly lit storefronts flash past. Nestled against the river, this once thriving mill town was making a comeback as an arts center. Christmas wreaths hung on lampposts, and white lights twinkled in the trees lining the sidewalk.

Following the river road out of town, they soon reached the seaside village and ascended the bluff to the SeaMount Agency's headquarters. On the horizon, the winter sun sank into the ocean.

"Oh!" Talia's hand flew to her mouth. She stared at the peak of the building.

At the highest point, several men dressed in cammies and red Santa hats dangled from ropes. The wind off the ocean whipped at their clothing and the loose strands of Christmas lights.

"Late in the day to still be up there." Ethan shook his head.

"They *say* they're racing to finish for the open house." Charlie glanced over his shoulder grinning. "I believe the hurry has more to do with Aggie's wassail than actually flipping the switch on the lights." Pulling into the half circle drive at the front of the building, he stopped the SUV at the bottom of the steps leading to the double front doors.

Not the entrance normally used by the men, Ethan nodded his thanks before helping Talia from the vehicle.

She stared up at the yellow building trimmed in white

gingerbread. "It's a Victorian hotel." The wind ruffled the end of her scarf.

"It was." Ethan held her elbow and urged her up the flight of stone steps. "Sam razed the old building and rebuilt from the ground up using architectural pieces salvaged from the original." He hustled her through the double doors.

The patter of running feet mingled with high-pitched squeals. Two little girls burst into the room. The first was so fair her skin gave the impression of being translucent. Her blonde hair was almost white. The other girl's complexion was the color of dark honey. A cloud of black curls haloed her smiling face. Identical tiaras sparkled on the tops of their heads.

"Unca Ethan. Unca Ethan." In tandem they launched themselves at him.

Heart near bursting, he folded his arms around them. "How're my princesses?" He swung them in an exuberant circle. They shrieked, faces aglow with happiness.

Setting them on their feet, he studied Talia as each girl grabbed one of his hands. "Talia, meet Hanna and Angelina."

Chapter 6

Emotion constricted Talia's throat. Overwhelmed, she sank into the nearest overstuffed chair. Seeing Angelina's beaming face was like looking at a mirror image of herself at that age.

Dressed in a heavy sweatshirt and pants, the child clung to Ethan. Curiosity filled her big brown eyes.

Words eluded Talia.

Ethan rescued her. "Angelina, what did you and Hanna do today?"

"Made reindeer food!" Her island accent gave her words a clipped cadence.

"Reindeer food?" *Brilliant, Talia.* She looked at Ethan for help.

"Show us."

The girls ran off in the direction they'd come from.

Ethan held out his hand. His gentle smile caused a soft trembling in Talia's belly. Flustered, she clasped the hand he offered.

He led her past a baby grand piano to a wide doorway where a flamboyant orchid held center stage on a large round pedestal. Beyond it, the dining room that overlooked the ocean could have been in a five star hotel. Round tables were set with beautiful china and glassware.

"What a lovely room." The spicy scent of tomato sauce wafted through the air. Talia's stomach curled with hunger. Ethan had offered her lunch in the train's dining car, but she'd been too nervous to eat.

He waved his hand to encompass the entire room. "Aggie believes the fancy stuff keeps us civilized. She's convinced without her intervention we'd degenerate into an adult frat house."

The girls climbed onto high chairs at the counter separating the dining room from the kitchen. It looked as though a container of steel cut oats had exploded all over the granite surface. Gumdrops, mini marshmallows, and sparkly jimmies peppered the drifts of grain.

Each girl held up a bowl.

Talia peeked inside both. "Reindeer eat that?"

"*Santa's* reindeer." Hanna stirred her bowl with a giant spoon, flipping more bits onto the counter. Clearly, she thought Talia knew diddly about feeding magical reindeer.

Talia picked up a marshmallow. "It's the sugar." To survive the moment, she jumped into the children's world with both feet. *Like visiting Papa.* "I'm sure this food will help Santa's reindeer make their trip around the world."

Angelina and Hanna grinned and stirred all the harder, convinced Santa's reindeer would run out of steam if they didn't do their part.

Charlie entered the dining room shedding his coat. "Your luggage is in your suite."

A tiny woman bustled out of the pantry at the rear of the kitchen and stopped short. A strand of gray hair dangled from her bun. "You're here! Someone should'a told me." She pushed past the men to reach Talia. "My, you're a tall one."

"Talia, meet Aggie." Ethan landed a peck on Aggie's wrinkled cheek. "She's our resident tyrant."

Aggie shooed him away. "You men help the little ones clean up the mess." She waved a hand in Talia's direction. "Come with me."

Not sure what to make of this diminutive woman, Talia fell into step behind her.

"You take a minute before supper to freshen up." Aggie led her to an elevator and jabbed a button. "I'm glad you're here. Time I was back in my own bed. Fresh sheets are on yours. The children are expecting you. Don't know you're their aunt, though." She faced Talia. "You have a difficult decision to make."

Talia's heart skipped a beat and trepidation flooded through her as she followed Aggie into the elevator.

"We don't dress fancy for meals. May look classy, but its family style. Don't let the men intimidate you." Aggie continued to rattle off information, including where to find the spa, the gym, and the lap pool. By the time they exited the elevator and arrived at their destination, Talia's head spun. She would never find her way back to the dining room, much less to any of the other places mentioned.

Aggie opened the door, and Talia stepped into the children's suite.

"Supper in half an hour." Aggie closed the door leaving her alone.

Surrounded by the beige tones of sand and sea, the hard knot inside Talia started to unravel. She had expected an impersonal place of business with guests relegated to a hotel. Instead, she found herself in the re-creation of a grand Victorian building—both home and business center for the SeaMount Agency.

Standing before the floor to ceiling windows overlooking

the ocean, she watched the setting sun paint an apricot streak across the horizon. Against the black of the water, lights winked indicating vessels on the move.

Talia rested her brow against the cool glass and closed her eyes. Meeting Angelina shook her resolve to make a dispassionate decision about the children. *Father God, what am I to do? What is* Your *will?* God's way was never easy or comfortable. He asked a great deal of His children, expecting them to depend on His wisdom and strength. If she were truly honest with herself, she already knew the answer to her question. She sighed. Like Moses, she felt unprepared for this venture.

Chapter 7

Ethan stood on the deck embracing the cold wind blowing off the ocean. Waves tumbled ashore, their turmoil mirroring the emotional upheaval crashing over him.

If he believed in wishes, he'd make one now on the low hanging star twinkling in the purple dusk of the sky. He'd ask for one more glimpse of Lacey. It had become harder to remember the many details of their years together. Details he had promised himself he'd never forget.

Running feet thudded across the lower deck. Voices drifted on the wind. In the glow of recessed lights, Davie and Simao goofed around on the wide steps that led down to the lawn. To ward off the chill of the northern climate, Simao wore a heavy coat, gloves, and a knit cap pulled down over his ears.

The familiar wash of fatherliness flooded Ethan's chest. The first time he'd laid eyes on Simao was on the island of St. Beatrice. He'd known immediately this was the child in his reoccurring dreams—dreams that were not random because God did nothing by chance.

Scrubbing a hand over his face, he cast one last glance toward heaven before stepping indoors.

Sam waited for him in the hall. "Come with me." As the driving force behind SeaMount, Sam handpicked the men who worked for him. He expected one hundred percent loyalty.

Ethan followed his boss into the Club Room. The small fireplace, faced with decorative Italian tiles, flickered brightly. Ethan leaned an elbow on the wood mantle and waited.

Sam lowered his frame into a winged back chair and rested his leg on the ottoman. "How did Ms. Combs receive the news?"

Ethan shook his head. "She'd been told her mother died when she was an infant. She didn't know she had a sister." He understood her anger. That news alone was enough to rock her well-ordered world. Adding a nephew and niece to the mix was the final blow. Her world was knocked off its axis. He was still amazed she'd agreed to accompany him to Rhode Island. "Her father is in an Alzheimer's unit and unable to answer her questions." Stuffing his hands in his pockets, Ethan described the classroom confrontation and his part in securing the teen.

Sam ran his forefinger across his bushy mustache. "Has Talia given any indication she's prepared to take her sister's children?"

"No. She was quiet on the ride here. Not what I'd expected."

Sam's eyes narrowed. "If she chooses not to take them, other arrangements will have to be made."

The bottom dropped out of Ethan's stomach. "Give her time." *Surely she'd do the right thing given enough time.*

"Simao is a bright kid. He may hear one of the adults say something about his relationship to Talia. I don't want him finding out by accident. And take care around Davie. Those two boys are thick as thieves." The director cracked a smile. "Maybe not the best expression to use in this case. Just keep an eye on them." He rubbed a hand along his thigh. "What one doesn't know the other is more than willing to teach."

"Yes, sir." Davie was Sam's special project. The boy's father had saved Sam from certain death at the cost of losing his own life. Sam was determined his savior's son would grow up outside the penal system.

Hoisting himself out of the chair, Sam limped to the door. "I want Simao and Angelina to know Talia is their aunt before the neighbors come for the open house. Make it happen."

Chapter 8

The door to her suite burst open. Talia spun around. A young boy ran into the room and came to an abrupt halt. Surprise raced across his dark features.

Talia smiled. "Hello, I'm Talia. What's your name?" Out of her element, she couldn't assume he was her nephew.

Playing with the doorknob, his feet shuffled in place. "Simao Rivas. Are you here to take care of us?"

"Aggie has many duties." Talia stepped away from the window. "So here I am." She held out her hand.

His dark gaze inspected her as though taking her measure. For someone so young, his eyes were shadowed with secrets, as though he'd seen too much in his short life. He stepped forward and shook her hand. Like his sister, he was dressed in several warm layers.

"Come sit with me, Simao, and tell me about your trip to SeaMount."

Gingerly, he sat at her side on the couch. He started to lift his sneakered feet up on to the cushion but stopped midway as if remembering his manners.

"Did you fly in an airplane?"

Hands clasped between his knees, he nodded. "Miss Ava told us what to do."

"Who's Miss Ava?"

His face brightened into a genuine smile. "We stayed with her in a house before coming here. She was our teacher."

"What did she teach you?"

"How to talk English better...and manners." Apprehension stole his smile. "She said we would start a new life and be happy."

"And are you happy?"

He ducked his head. "Angelina is happy."

Talia reached for his hand and squeezed it. "Give yourself some time." *Listen to your own advice, Talia.* She took a deep breath. "This place is huge. Can you show me the way back to the dining room?"

He rose, grabbed her hand and pulled her off the couch.

"Ooo!"

Heading for the door, he tugged her along in his wake.

Talia careened across the room. "I haven't met everyone yet." She flung her hand out to keep from running into an occasional table. "When we arrived," she sucked in a breath, "men on ropes were stringing Christmas lights." Bouncing off the door jam, she grabbed the knob and pulled the door shut as they flew through.

She hoped she survived to eat dinner in that lovely dining room.

Talia's entrance into the room brimming with boisterous men was not graceful. Simao had insisted the elevator was too slow, so they'd descended three flights of stairs at a breakneck pace.

Breathless, she grasped the edge of the counter and plopped onto a high chair. She must have appeared in need of rescuing because Ethan headed her way. His easy smile caused her heart to pang. The children weren't the only ones playing havoc with her emotions.

"Simao, round up your sister." He placed Talia's hand in the crook of his arm.

She was thankful for his presence at her side as he escorted her farther into the room thick with alpha males.

The first man she met wore a sling and went by the odd name of Preach. The next two men, Gabe and Logan St. John, were twins. Telling them apart would be a challenge. With each introduction she was faced with a probing gaze.

Her pulse tripped. What if she didn't measure up? Would they send her away without the children? *And why does that thought send you into a panic? You aren't even sure you want to take them!* She dropped into the chair Ethan held for her. Angelina and Hanna sat on her left. Ethan and Simao claimed seats on her right.

"Hanna is the daughter of an agent living off site. She's stayed here to help Angelina with the transition." Ethan's soft words were for Talia's ears only.

A tall cowboy approached carrying a pan of bubbling lasagna. He set the dish on the hot mat in the center of the table. Tipping his hat in Talia's direction, he dropped into the empty seat between Hanna and Simao. He stowed the hat beneath his chair. "You're the woman Sam was searching for."

Ethan stiffened. "McCord."

The warning note wasn't lost on the cowboy. He glanced at the children, and then at Ethan before his sharp green eyes rested on Talia. "I'm Whit McCord. How's New York City?"

Biting her lip to suppress a giggle, Talia cleared her throat. "Big." The entrance of another man saved her from having to elaborate.

"That's the director, Sam Traven." Ethan's warm breath fanned Talia's ear.

"Preach, please say grace." The director's voice was as rough as the topography of his face. Sometime in the past, he'd endured injuries that left him horribly scarred.

Amazed that these strong, self-sufficient men felt the need to have a relationship with a sovereign God, Talia bowed her head.

Preach's prayer was brief. It was followed by a lone baritone voice singing the first few words of the Doxology before all the men joined in.

Talia let the mellow harmony of tenor, baritone, and bass voices weave through the chaotic emotions that had held her captive for the past two days. As the last notes faded, she sighed. The tension she'd carried since the incident in her classroom melted away.

"You okay?" Ethan's whisper tickled her ear.

"That was beautiful. Do you always sing at the table?"

"When the mood strikes one of us."

The moment was followed by a groundswell of animated conversation, a sharp contrast to Talia's usual quiet meals.

Aggie wove between tables refilling breadbaskets and checking on the children. Whit snagged her apron string, and the bow untied as she walked away. Winking at Talia, he dug into his plate piled high with pasta.

A teenage boy snuck up behind Simao. "Hey, Squirt."

Lunging out of his chair, Simao wrapped his arms around the teen's skinny waist.

"Yo, man. Leave me standing."

"Davie, sit and mind your manners."

At Whit's reprimand, the teen pushed Simao back into the chair then nudged him over until they sat hip to hip on the seat.

Talia waited for one of the men to correct the situation, but they appeared oblivious. The teen picked up Simao's spoon and began to eat off her nephew's plate. *Was this the normal arrangement for the two of them?* Simao looked happy enough.

Aggie approached and plunked a place setting in front of Davie. "You're not a hobo eating from a communal pot, young man."

Not looking the least bit chastened, he filled his own plate but remained seated with Simao.

"He's put on weight," Ethan murmured.

She studied the child. Even bundled in heavy clothing, he was rail thin.

A tiny hand patted Talia's forearm, and her heart flip-flopped.

Tomato sauce smeared Angelina's chin. A crumb of bread dotted her eyebrow. "Here, sweetie, let me help you." Using a napkin, Talia gently wiped Angelina's face. An unexpected rush of heat welled in her chest. *How did this sweet baby survive on the street with only her brother, a child himself, to watch over her?*

Talia's heart throbbed and shifted. Tears pooled in her eyes, and the angelic face blurred. The desire to pull Angelina into her arms surged through her, but fear froze her in place. *What if the child pushed her away? What if everyone in the room, including the children, read too much into the action?* There were so many things to consider...her career...her father....

Trust me.

The Spirit's whisper resonated in Talia's soul. *I want to trust.* But her heart held onto the fear that, in this moment, loomed larger than her faith.

Chapter 9

Ethan ignored the elevator and ran up the stairs to Talia's suite in the guest wing.

Following supper, Sam had called the men together for a briefing. A request for security support had come in from a firm in Central America.

Bedtime for the little ones was fast approaching, and Ethan hoped to say goodnight. *Keep telling yourself this is just about the kids, Thomas. Maybe you'll believe it at some point.*

Simao answered Ethan's knock on the door dressed in blue pajamas and holding a book. Before Ethan could ask what he was reading, a chorus of muffled shrieks rang out. Sweeping him aside, Ethan sprinted into the room. "*Talia*?"

Behind the bathroom door high-pitched squeals accompanied the low rumble of air jets.

"No! No more!" Panic edged Talia's voice.

Giving the door one warning pound with his fist, Ethan turned the knob. He charged in hitting a knee-high wall of bubbles before skidding three feet. Grabbing a corner of the vanity, he slowed his abrupt entrance.

Talia swung around, eyes wide with alarm. Bubbles, like those billowing from the tub, covered the front of her sweater. "I can't find the OFF button." Bracelets tinkling, she pawed through the suds.

Reaching around her to the rear corner, he found the button and silenced the jets. Two cherubic faces peered at him from the cloud of foam.

Talia sat on the closed lid of the toilet. "They added shampoo...." Her bemused voice trailed off. The blob of bubbles perched in her hair trembled each time she moved.

"We're *clean.*" Hanna tossed a handful of foam into the air.

To hide her smile, Talia lifted a sudsy hand to her lips then, realizing her folly, snatched it away.

Ethan's heart jumped before landing, feeling lighter than it had in two years. Relieved she saw the humor in the situation, he pointed to the shower in the opposite corner of the room. "How about you rinse them off while I call for help."

"Thank you." She grabbed a towel from the rack. "Okay, girls. We've finished tubby time."

Before leaving, Ethan glanced over his shoulder at Talia wiping bubbles from faces and hair. His nape tingled as if he were the one feeling her gentle caress. He forced himself to close the door behind him.

Simao waited just outside the bathroom door, his face pinched in a worried frown. His fingers plucked at the hem of his shirt. "I will help clean."

"Thank you. I'll call Charlie and get some mops up here."

The youngster followed close on Ethan's heels waiting while the call was made. The minute Ethan finished Simao spoke. "Do we have to go away?" He glanced at the closed bathroom door.

Ethan's heart ached. "No. From now on you will always have a home, Simao." That promise was not his to make.

Talia held first claim on this boy and his sister. *Lord, let her do the right thing.* Ethan rubbed his hands together. *Was he anxious because he didn't want to be faced with the choice...or because he knew in his bones what he would ultimately decide?*

A racket arose in the hall. Opening the door, Ethan found the entire team armed with mops.

Whit was lead instigator. "Hear there's water that needs mopping. Problems with your plumbing, Thomas?"

Laughter mingled with a few ribald comments. Apparently the bubble calamity was the evening's entertainment for this bunch of boneheads. He stepped aside to let them enter.

The bathroom door swung open. Wrapped in towels, Angelina and Hanna raced through the sitting room and into the small bedroom. Talia followed, gawking at the crowd of men as she scrambled to keep up with her charges.

Acting like spectators at a race, the men cheered them on.

Swabbing the floor took the next hour. The bathroom wasn't large enough to easily accommodate so many men more interested in hijinks than with helping. They included Simao in the fun, and amid the joking and laughter, the bubbles and water disappeared, and Simao's smile returned.

Later that night Ethan sat on the edge of his bed. Elbows on his knees, he hunched forward praying through the events of the day. He cradled a tiny handcrafted angel in his hands. A narrow strip of old quilt wrapped its wooden peg body. Colorful thread edged a heart shaped quilt scrap that, attached to the angel's back, became wings.

At Lacey and Josh's funeral, an elderly parishioner placed the angel in Ethan's hand. The woman didn't say a word. She simply folded his fingers around it never knowing what she'd given him. Raw with grief, the little angel became a special part of his evening prayers.

Ethan traced the edge of the heart-shaped wings with his thumb. His visions, and every divine appointment the world labeled a coincidence, were under God's control. He absolutely believed this. But tonight, his preoccupation with Talia, Simao, and Angelina weighed on him like a betrayal to the family he'd lost.

With the tiny angel warming his hand, Ethan bowed his head and poured out his confusion to his Lord and Savior.

Chapter 10

High on ladders, Talia and Gray Kerr hung a wreath on the beach stone fireplace.

"Turn it a little to the right." Gray's wife, Sophie stood at the foot of his ladder.

He followed orders, a hint of a smile sliding across his somber features.

"That's perfect."

Talia stepped off her ladder and looked at their handiwork. White lights, shiny red balls, and an enormous red velvet bow decorated the balsam wreath. It was traditional and perfect for the setting.

"Let's decorate the railing and stairs next." Sophie gave her husband a quick kiss that he happily returned. "We can do this ourselves. Go help the men with the lights."

His face brightened and after another quick smooch, he sprinted for the door.

Sophie grinned at Talia.

Talia returned her look, and they both burst into laughter.

"Thank you for letting Hanna stay with Angelina." Talia's bracelets jingled as she stuffed the lush garland of laurel between balusters and wrapped it up and over the rail.

Sophie followed her, using the same motions to

intertwine tiny white lights through the shiny leaves. "I thought she'd be more comfortable with another little girl by her side. To Hanna and her two sisters, all the men are honorary uncles. They grant their every wish. But, to someone who doesn't know them, the men can be as overwhelming as this building."

Talia paused in her tucking and pulling, "They are and it is."

Sophie smiled. "I felt the same way when I stayed here."

Surprise zinged through Talia. "You stayed here?"

"At one time my home was uninhabitable. Sam insisted we stay here." A tiny smile tipped the corners of Sophie's lips. "The building is huge, and they call it 'headquarters.' But make no mistake, this place is also a home."

Talia fluffed the waxy laurel leaves. Less than forty-eight hours at SeaMount headquarters and already she felt as though she'd come home. *Which makes no sense at all.* She owned a nice home in the city.

"Looking good." Ethan hurried past. The pom pom on his Santa hat bounced with each step.

Sophie whispered, "I think he meant you."

Heat infused Talia's cheeks. "I'm sure he meant the decorations." But she couldn't suppress the smile twitching on her lips.

Working the lights into the foliage to hide the wire, Sophie knelt for better access. "He's a widower."

Talia's hands stilled as her curiosity got the better of her. "What happened?"

Sophie stopped what she was doing and sat back on her heels. "Two years ago he was still active duty—not working for Sam—and home on leave. His wife and son had gone shopping." Sophie's voice roughened. "There was a huge accident on the highway. It involved many cars.

Unfortunately, Ethan's wife and son were part of it and were killed."

Knees trembling, Talia slid to the floor. "How awful," she whispered past the lump in her throat.

Sophie smoothed her fingertips over the strand of lights she held. "My heart goes out to him. I lost a spouse, too."

Talia stared at her. "You?"

"Yes. I had the girls with my first husband. Gray loves them like they're his own."

Am I capable of loving Simao and Angelina like they are my own? With fumbling fingers Talia adjusted the sweep of the garland. *Or will they be nothing more than constant reminders of the family I've lost?*

Chapter 11

Leaning into the wind, Talia walked with Ethan along the flagstone path that stretched across the winter brown lawn. Behind them, Simao and Angelina leapt from one stone to the next.

The blanket of dark clouds tumbling overhead matched Talia's mood. Not even this morning's church service succeeded in lifting her spirit. She shot a quick sideways glance at Ethan. How did he carry on day after day without his family? The longing to visit Papa weighed heavy on her heart after only a few days.

Arriving at the greenhouse where Sam indulged his passion for raising orchids, Ethan opened the door and stepped aside to let her and the children pass.

One step over the threshold and the atmosphere changed from blustery cold to tropical warmth. Talia breathed in the pungent scent of damp bark and moss. Rows of low, wire mesh benches held the potted orchids. An occasional delicate blossom dotted the expanse of green.

"Ohh." Simao snatched off his hat and let it drop to the floor. His gloves and coat followed. Eyes closed, he inhaled. "Like home."

Talia's stomach dropped and landed with the low boom of

a bass drum. Of course he missed the island's warm climate.

Angelina ran down the aisle toward the back of the building. The soles of her shoes *tap-tapped* over the cement floor, past rows of pots and trellises that supported climbing orchids.

Talia caught up to her just as she reached the corner where the life-size nativity figures were stored.

"Baby Jesus." Angelina patted the small figure in the crude wooden manger. With childish adoration, she stroked the plastic face and kissed the painted cheek.

Ethan and Simao joined them, and Talia flashed a watery smile. "Angelina found baby Jesus."

Brow creased with uncertainty, Ethan's gaze bounced between her tear-filled eyes and trembling lips.

"Mary, Joseph and Jesus." Simao pointed in turn to each figure. "And three kings."

Understanding lit Ethan's eyes. "Simao, who told you about baby Jesus and the three kings?"

"Mama told us."

Ethan held his hand out to Simao. "Come tell us about Christmas on the island." He led the boy to a park bench strategically placed among the plant tables.

Talia sat at one end of the bench with Angelina on her lap. Simao squeezed in between the adults. Over her nephew's head she mouthed "*Thank you*" to Ethan.

The boy scuffed his shoes on the cement floor. "Papa Noel visited on Christmas night. But not after Mama died. He didn't know where to find us."

Ethan patted the boy's knee. "He'll find you this year, Simao."

"And Angelina, too?"

"Yes. Angelina, too."

Sadness for the children welled up in Talia's chest. It

clogged her throat making speech impossible. Thankfully, Ethan had no such problem.

"Did your mother and grandmother do anything special to celebrate Christmas?"

Afraid to breathe lest she miss a word, Talia pressed her lips into Angelina's curls.

"They cleaned the house at Christmas." Simao rolled his eyes. "Everything *clean*."

Talia gasped. She did the same! She polished furniture and replaced curtains in preparation for the holiday. Her voice rasped as she asked, "What was your favorite part of Christmas, Simao?"

His face lit up. "Bamboo bursting." He erupted from the seat. Arms flung wide, he made an explosive sound.

Ethan grinned. "I've heard of that. Like firing a cannon. They vaporize kerosene and *kaboom*." He frowned. "The bamboo must be big."

With his fingers, Simao formed a circle six inches in diameter.

An impression of peril niggled at Talia's conscience. "Sounds dangerous."

Both males offered an identical shrug of their shoulder.

Intuition sounded an alarm in her mind. "What causes the fuel to vaporize?"

They exchanged a secretive look and clamped their lips shut.

"Tell me or I'll search for the answer on the Internet."

"Fire."

Definitely dangerous. Thankfully bamboo did not grow to the requisite size in this part of the world. "What other things did you do to celebrate?"

"The Masquerade. Everyone wears costumes, and they dance and sing in the streets."

"Like *carnivale*?"

He nodded. "But at Masquerade the Wild Cow and Horse Head chase us."

Talia's heart beat hard against her ribs. Droplets of perspiration bloomed across her brow. She fought the darkness edging her vision.

"Talia?" Ethan's voice reached her from far away. "Talia what is it?"

She forced her gaze to meet his. "My dream. A terrible dream I've had since I was little." Her dry mouth made speaking difficult. "What if it isn't a dream, but...."

Ethan placed his hand on her shoulder. "A memory?"

She wasn't sure. "I'm terrified and running from a giant ugly horse. My shoes pinch my feet." *Had they been new for Christmas?*

Simao's eyes lit with interest. "You saw the Masquerade?"

Tell him now.

The still, small voice startled her. *Now, Lord?* In her chest, a knot of fear tightened.

Fear not.

Afraid to trust God's timing, but even more fearful she'd miss a divinely orchestrated opportunity, she glanced at Ethan. He smiled in encouragement.

"Yes." She gulped. "Yes, I believe I must have." She tightened her arms around the little girl nestled on her lap. "I was Angelina's age...maybe younger. I was born on St. Beatrice, Simao. I'm... I'm your aunt."

Simao's smile wavered then collapsed into an anguished grimace. He buried his face in his hands and sobbed.

Panic arrowed through Talia. This was not the response she'd expected.

Ethan wrapped his arms around the boy as though trying to hold him together. "Why does that news hurt, Simao?"

"She cried for you."

"Who cried?" Ethan frowned. "Your mama?"

Simao shook his head.

"Your grandmother?"

"Yeesss."

Simao's revelation pierced Talia's heart. Regret added its weight to the sadness bearing down on her. Strong arms encircled her and Angelina. Simao was squished in the middle of Ethan's hug.

"She wanted you to come. Her other daughter." Simao's shoulders heaved. "She did not speak your name."

Talia covered her eyes with her hands. Hot tears flowed unchecked. "I-I didn't know she was alive."

Upset by Simao and Talia's distress, Angelina whimpered.

Simao hiccupped and scrubbed at his eyes with his fists. "When she was sick I helped her."

Talia curled an arm around Simao. "I would have come. If I'd known, I would have come." She rested her chin on the top of his head. Closing her eyes, she opened her heart. *Father, taking these children as my own is a huge step. You're sure I can do this alone? Maybe you can send me someone to help? Someone like Ethan?* The unexpected thought made her heart bounce hard. Her eyes popped open. Warm brown eyes captured her gaze.

Chapter 12

Ethan held Talia, Simao, and Angelina against his chest. He thanked God for arms long enough and a heart big enough to absorb the tumult of emotions that rocketed through the three of them.

Talia stared at him, her eyes bright with tears. He grazed her damp cheek with his knuckles, and her eyelids fluttered.

Against his side, Simao stirred.

Ethan loosened his hold. The reluctance in Talia's eyes matched his own as he pulled away. "Ready to set up the manger scene?"

Ever resilient, Simao hopped off the bench. "Now?"

"Yes. Put your coats on." Ethan stood and offered Talia his hand. The glow in her eyes, so much like his vision of her beneath the water, stole his breath. Only after inhaling, slow and deep, was he able to speak again. "Angelina may carry baby Jesus."

After much discussion, and several trips between the greenhouse and the patch of grass in the center of the half circle driveway, the nativity was assembled. Angelina and Simao were scattering hay at the feet of the three kings and the camel when the first snowflakes drifted from the sky. Captivated by the scene they'd helped create, they didn't notice.

Then a cold gust of wind brought a thick sweep of snow.

The children froze in place. Icy crystals peppered their cheeks. Simao lifted his face to the sky, eyes wide with wonder.

Angelina screeched in fear and threw herself at Talia.

"Ooh, sweetie." Talia hugged her close. "That's snow. It doesn't hurt."

Angelina buried her face in Talia's scarf.

"Snow?" Arms raised, Simao lifted his face to the sky and spun in a tight circle. "Does snow fall everywhere like rain? Is this a blizzard?"

Ethan laughed. "No, this is not a blizzard." The child had a lot to learn. "We're finished here. If we ask nice, maybe Aggie'll make hot chocolate and feed us Christmas cookies."

He caught Talia watching him, and warmth rushed through his chest. Snowflakes landed on her eyelashes as she rocked side-to-side soothing Angelina. From an inner source, her beautiful face radiated peace—something he longed for in the dark hours of the night. Was he willing to pay the price? Did he have the courage to tell her everything?

The foaming curl of the wave boiled around Ethan as he rode it to shore. The drysuit and warm undergarment he wore protected him from the cold Atlantic Ocean. In the shallows, he removed his fins and waded out of the water. High on the bluff, headquarters glowed in the early morning sunlight. He crossed the wind-rippled sand and stepped onto the boardwalk leaving the other men to finish putting in their time before following him ashore.

Descending the tiled steps into the locker room, he set his

fins and gloves in the rinse trough. He stripped off his hood and suit and hosed them down in the tank before hanging them to dry. Stepping out of the warm undergarment, he entered the shower room. A motion-activated showerhead rained hot water like stinging darts against his cool skin. One by one the other men showed up, their voices and the splash of water bouncing off the tiled walls.

He left the steamy room and found Preach standing at the rinse trough spraying fresh water over the booties and fins. "Thanks."

"You're welcome." With one arm permanently out of commission, Preach no longer trained with the team. He hooked the nozzle out of the way and turned to face Ethan. "Been watching you."

Ethan pulled on his jeans. Shirt in hand, he slammed the door of his locker. "Yeah?"

"Something about you is off." Intent blue eyes issued an unwavering challenge.

Stubborn anger tore through Ethan. The man saw way too much. "That so."

"You ignoring God?" Preach tweaked his arm bound in a sling. "Been there, done that. Believe me when I say, He'll get your attention."

Padding barefoot across the room, Ethan shrugged into his shirt. "You forgetting *I'm* the one with a hot line to heaven?"

"Yeah, well, by the look on your face, nobody's answering on the other end."

Ethan pulled on his socks and stuffed his feet in his shoes. Last night Talia had spoken with Sam. She told him the children knew of their relationship to her. What she'd do now was anyone's guess.

Preach stretched his leg and spoke Ethan's thoughts

aloud. "What if Talia won't take them? You going to be okay with them going into the home Sam and I are getting up and running?"

No! Ethan yanked on his shoestring. It broke leaving him holding the ragged end. He stared at it feeling like he was at his own ragged end.

"Or," Preach kept talking, "we could skip that step, and you could give them what they need."

The statement speared through Ethan. *Surely she will take them.* He dropped the shoestring and buttoned his shirt with shaking hands. Another family to love...and risk losing? *God, help me.*

Stepping into the lower foyer Ethan paused. The *splosh splosh* of Sam swimming laps in the pool mingled with the sweet sound of "Away In A Manger" being played on the piano.

Ethan stopped at the bottom of the stairs to listen. Over the course of the week, Talia had sat at the keyboard and played many times. He'd begun to know her moods by the music she chose, and her execution of the piece. Wistfulness threaded through the children's Christmas hymn. Was she remembering another Christmas from her childhood? He powered up the steps two at a time. Close to the top he peered through the decorated balusters.

Her hands hovered over the ivory keys. Her touch was light, the notes delicate. Eyes closed, her body swayed to the rhythm of the music.

Bang! A rattling crash came from the kitchen.

Ethan bound to the top of the stairs and sprinted toward the sound.

Aggie stood on a stool in front of the cupboard where she stored her baking pans. Several cookie sheets lay scattered on the floor.

Talia nudged Ethan aside. Stepping over pans, she took Aggie's hand. "Are you okay?"

"'Course I'm okay."

Ethan picked up the heavy pan closest to the stool. "Next time ask for help."

"That's my special pan for the gingerbread house." With their help, she climbed down.

He hefted the cast aluminum mold. "When you're finished, let one of us put this away for you."

Talia collected the other pans and placed them on the counter of the industrial dishwasher. "May I help you bake?"

"Nope." Aggie took the mold Ethan held. "Open house is tomorrow night. Time to get the Christmas tree." She swished her hands as though shooing chickens. "Go on. Pick us a good one."

It wasn't long and they had the children properly dressed and corralled in the rear seat of the SUV. Heading inland to the Christmas tree farm, Ethan and Talia took turns fielding the questions coming from the peanut gallery.

Yes, you can help choose the tree. No, you cannot climb it.

For the first time in two years Ethan felt whole. *Like part of a family.* The thought washed over him with startling clarity.

The horse-drawn hay wagon left Simao speechless with wonder. Ethan steadied Talia as she climbed on board then handed up the children. Simao waded through the hay making a beeline to the front of the wagon. Finding his voice, he peppered the driver with questions. Angelina plopped herself in the center of the wagon bed and tossed a handful of hay in the air. Chaff dotted her red knit hat.

The children's happiness caused Ethan's heart to squeeze.

Talia placed a hand on his shoulder. "Are you all right?"

"Yeah. Hay in my eye." Placing his boot on the metal step, he climbed in.

Talia scooted over and propped her back against the sideboard.

Folding his legs, Ethan sat beside her, careful to keep space between them.

The wagon swayed, and harness bells jingled in time to the *clop clop* of the horses' hooves.

Ethan breathed in the sharp scent of balsam to clear his head. He glanced at Talia. A corkscrew curl had escaped her knit hat and fluttered against her brow. Clenching his hands into fists, he refused to give into the urge to touch. "Talia." He spoke before he could talk himself out of saying what was on his mind. "I was married before." *Why was he telling her that? Idiot!*

"I know. Sophie told me."

His vision tunneled on her, all senses on alert.

She concentrated on the zipper pull on his jacket. "We weren't gossiping. She told me when we were decorating the sitting room."

Why did this revelation please him so much? "She told you about my wife, Lacey, and my son, Joshua?" Even in the worst firefight of his career, his heart hadn't hammered this hard.

"Yes."

He couldn't help himself. He reached out and grasped her

hand. But mitten and glove prevented him from feeling the warmth of her palm. Regret speared through him. He wanted to say more. Sophie didn't know everything. No one did but him. He'd chosen to never share, instead holding the precious secret close to his heart.

"Whoooa." The wagon stopped, and the driver swiveled in his seat. He gestured toward the Balsam firs on both sides of the road. "All of them, between ten and fifteen feet tall."

Jumping off the wagon, Ethan reached for Talia. Even with the layers of clothing she wore, her waist was small in the circle of his hands. Her mittens rested feather light on his shoulders. He lifted her down—and held on. His breath hitched. He fell into the deep mystery of her eyes with no thought of saving himself.

Thump thump. Something soft whacked the back of his head. He looked over his shoulder.

Angelina's mittened hand was raised and ready to deliver another soft bop.

He released his hold on Talia and swung Angelina off the wagon in a dizzying swoop that made her squeal.

Enchanted by the proximity of so many Christmas trees in their natural habitat, Simao jumped off the wagon and sped away.

"Stay close." Setting Angelina on her feet, Ethan held her tiny hand in his. Talia grasped her niece's other hand.

With energy to spare, Simao darted in and out of the trees lined up like soldiers in formation. They caught up to him as he circled one particular tree brushing his hands through the dense green needles.

"This one?" His smile was tentative.

"Let's see." Ethan walked around the tree. "Looks tall enough. Nice and round, too. Aggie has a special star ornament for the spire on top." He studied the slender tip.

Making the moment a solemn occasion, Ethan handed Simao the red tag. "You found the perfect tree. You may do the honors of marking it."

Simao carefully wound the wire around the branch. He flashed his bright smile and without warning launched himself at Ethan.

Ethan raised his hands—in defense, or maybe to catch him—he wasn't sure which. Either way, his arms ended up around the boy. "Merry Christmas, Simao."

"Merry Christmas." Ethan's coat muffled Simao's voice.

With the tree tagged, Simao was ready for the next part of the adventure—exploring the North Pole Gift Shop. Red poinsettias and wreaths aglitter with ornaments drew Angelina like magnets. Leaving her in Talia's care, Ethan grabbed a hand basket.

Simao stood in the center of an aisle surrounded by hundreds of glistening, shimmering, twinkling baubles. At his sides, his hands fluttered, and his fingers twitched.

Ethan rubbed a hand across his mouth. Simao had come a long way, but old survival skills died hard. This crowded shop could tempt the most reformed pickpocket. "Simao." He held out the basket. "Chose an ornament for your sister, and one for Aunt Talia. We'll pay for them at the counter."

Simao cast a longing glance at the car ornaments hanging on a nearby tree.

"And, you may choose an ornament for yourself."

"Any one I want?"

"That's right."

A great deal of thought went into each choice. Some time later Simao set the basket on the checkout counter. He paid for the ornaments with money Ethan slipped him. Eyes bright with pride, he carried his bag of ornaments from the store.

They found Talia and Angelina at a picnic table sipping hot chocolate and munching apple cider doughnuts.

"Here you go, men." Talia handed Ethan a hot chocolate before helping Simao with his. "There are more doughnuts in the bag."

After they'd eaten and disposed of the trash, Ethan announced the last stop on the adventure. "Let's go visit Santa." Ears ringing with happy shrieks, he plucked Angelina off the bench seat and settled her in the crook of his arm.

A short walk along a winding path of peppermint candy steppingstones led them to Santa's workshop. Thankfully, the line to meet the jolly elf was short. Soon Angelina sat on Santa's knee gently *pat-patting* his snowy beard.

"Have you been good this year?" Santa handed her a candy cane.

"Say 'yes,' Angelina," Simao coached his sister in a loud whisper.

"Ah, is that your brother?" Santa motioned to Simao. "Come here. Come join Angelina."

Suddenly less bold, Simao glanced at Talia.

She nodded her approval. "It's okay, Simao. Go ahead."

He approached Santa and placed a hand on the arm of the green velvet chair.

"What's on your Christmas list, Simao?"

"You know my name?"

Santa glanced at Talia, a twinkle in his blue eyes. "Ah. Santa knows many things."

Simao dipped his head. "You know who is good and who is bad." Each word dripped with disappointment.

Ethan's heart twisted. Was Simao remembering all he'd done on the island to survive? Stepping forward, he placed his hands on the boy's shoulders. "Santa grants new beginnings as well."

"Ho ho ho." A quick study, Santa took Simao's hand. "Indeed I do, young man." He peered at him over the top of his wire-rimmed glasses. "Tell me what you'd like for Christmas."

Simao held tight to the white-gloved hand. "I want a home with a mama and a papa."

Santa's merry blue eyes bounced between Talia and Ethan. "Ho ho ho."

Ethan's heart lurched. He had to save himself, as well as Santa. "Being united with your Aunt Talia is a good start, Simao." Surprised by the feminine hand slipping into the crook of his arm, he swung around. His gaze crash landed on Talia's soft mouth. He strained to hear her words through the roar in his ears.

"It's a wonderful beginning to your wish, Simao."

The boy studied Ethan and his aunt before returning his focus to Santa Claus. "I want Ethan to be my papa."

Simao's words seared across Ethan's heart. *No. He wasn't ready to love like that—so completely—again.* But a serious disconnect existed between the thoughts racing through his head and the emotions tumbling around in his heart. He glanced at Talia. The crinkled corners of her sparkling eyes signaled a smile hid behind her fuzzy mitten. Tongue dry as desert sand, he couldn't speak.

"What I want…. It's too much?" A note of sadness crept into Simao's voice.

Ethan's stomach dropped as Talia's hand tightened on his arm.

Santa's eyes lost a little of their twinkle. "You can never want too much love." He pinned first Talia, and then Ethan with his piercing blue eyes. "Your Aunt Talia and Ethan understand this." Patting Simao's shoulder, he smiled. "You are loved. As for the rest, let Christmas work its magic."

After that Ethan heard only a smattering of the conversation between the children and Santa. His heart and mind were in a no-holds-barred wrestling match.

"That's us." Talia shook his arm.

"What?"

"They announced our number. The tree is ready."

Thank you, Lord. Wondering how the woman had her wits about her, Ethan went through the motions of thanking Santa. He guided everyone through the crowd to the parking lot kiosk where their bundled tree waited.

Leaving Talia and the children there, Ethan sprinted for the SUV. He climbed in and leaned back against the headrest. Exhaling, he ran his hands over his face. He'd forgotten the minefields that existed in a relationship. He blew out a breath reminding himself he wasn't *in* a relationship. If that were to happen he would have to tell Talia his secrets. Would she understand? Hands trembling, he started the vehicle.

With the tree tied to the top of the car, they headed home. Snowflakes drifted from the sky, keeping the peanut gallery wound tight with excitement. Simao talked nonstop. His running commentary of the day continued even as Ethan drove the SUV into the half circle drive and stopped behind the Nativity.

Several of the men came out to help unload the tree. Simao bailed out of the vehicle happy to have new ears to assault.

Gabe released Angelina from her car seat and scooped her up.

Alone in the car with Talia, Ethan stuck a finger in his ear and wiggled it. "My eardrums are bleeding." Talia's breathy chuckle drew his gaze.

She stared at him over the folds of her purple scarf. "This

is the first time you've looked at me since leaving the farm."

"Yeah." Feeling silly, he pulled his finger out of his ear. "We need to talk."

"Yes. We do." She took a deep breath as though to say more.

"Not here." There were too many people, and there wasn't enough time for his liking. "Later. When we're alone."

Her gaze dipped to her lap where her mittened hands were clutched together. "Okay."

The strain in her voice brought him up short. In the chaos of his own inner battles, he'd given only a passing thought to the fact that he'd thrown her world off course when he'd shown up at her school.

Careful not to spook her, he placed his hand over hers. "With God's leading, it'll all fall into place." *Was he listening to his own words? Did he believe them?* He squeezed her hands. "Enjoy decorating the tree with the kids."

She drew a shaky breath. "Okay." A tentative smile wobbled across her lips. "Thank you for today."

He stretched across the console and pressed his lips to her cheeks. Heat blasted through him. He drew back, shockwaves quivering in his gut. She cupped his face with her hands. Her mittens tickled his skin.

"Tonight? Can we talk tonight?" Her eyes searched his face.

Having lost the ability to speak, he nodded.

"Thank you." She opened the car door and stepped out to join the others.

What had he done? What compelled him to kiss her? A knock on his window interrupted his whirling thoughts.

Whit grinned at him from the other side of the glass.

Ethan shoved open his door.

Whit jumped back, but his smile didn't waver. "You gonna help with the tree?"

Climbing out, Ethan threw the keys at him. "Make yourself useful and park it." He tailed after the crowd, his mind jumping ahead to this evening and the coming conversation with Talia.

Caressing where the warmth of Ethan's lips remained imprinted on her cheek, Talia stepped into the sitting room. The men were going about setting up the tree as though it were an engineering project. Angelina and Hanna danced with streamers of silver garland while Simao and Davie took orders from Aggie, bringing boxes of ornaments out of storage. Throughout the hubbub, the radar brought on by heightened awareness allowed Talia to follow Ethan's every move.

Tonight.

The word held a promise that sent tingles of anticipation up her arms. The tingles were followed by waves of anxiety crashing over her heart. His life was here. Her life was in the city. *Talia, stop it!*

To keep her thoughts from spinning out of control, she concentrated on removing ornaments from boxes. Like most family trees, they ranged from expensive, hand-painted glass to children's homemade offerings.

Once the decorating got underway in earnest, Aggie served apple cider and oatmeal cookies warm from the oven. One by one, the men lost interest and drifted away to relax in front of the crackling fire and relive past Christmases in faraway lands under less than ideal conditions.

Kneeling beside the tree, Talia helped Angelina hang the ornament Simao had bought for her—a marmalade kitten wearing a Santa's hat. Angelina promptly named the ornament "Pumpkin," and after much ado hooked it on a low hanging branch.

"This is for you, Aunt Tallie." Fidgeting, Simao held out a small bundle of tissue paper.

"You bought *me* an ornament?"

Her nephew nodded before glancing up at the man standing behind him.

Not daring to look at Ethan, Talia settled back on her heels and cupped the tissue paper in her hands. Tears burned behind her eyes. "Thank you."

The boisterous voices of Ethan's teammates faded as she peeled away the paper with trembling fingers. One last turn of the paper and the ornament rested in her palm. Her breath left her in a shaky sob. Unable to see through the tears spilling from her eyes, she cradled the precious golden heart in her hand.

"She doesn't like it?" Simao's worried question made Talia's heart squeeze.

In a low voice, Ethan reassured him. "Those are happy tears. She loves it too much to speak."

Grateful Ethan was there to explain, Talia blinked, furiously wanting to read the words on the fragile ornament.

I "heart" my wonderful aunt.

"It's lovely, Simao." She drew him close. "Thank you. I'll treasure this always." Her voice wobbled through each word. "Help me find the perfect spot on the tree."

Talia wiped the dampness from her cheeks. Her gaze got caught in the warm depths of Ethan's eyes, and her breath stalled in her chest.

Simao's Christmas wish was to have Ethan as his father.

We need to talk.

A timpani drum beat low in Talia's quivering tummy.

Chapter 13

Talia hurried down the boardwalk to the beachfront where the happy sound of Christmas carols being sung mingled with the boom of the waves. The annual open house was in full swing. Friends and neighbors had savored the indoor buffet, and she'd enjoyed taking requests and playing the piano for an appreciative audience. But the past twenty-four hours had been an emotionally draining roller coaster ride, and she just wanted the party to be over.

She and Ethan had never gotten the opportunity to talk last night.

Before the last ornament had been hung on the tree, Sam had summoned the men to the agency's control center hidden away in a far corner on the top floor. Supper and the children's bedtime had come and gone without the reappearance of any of the agents. Hours later, assured by Aggie this was not an uncommon occurrence, Talia had lowered the piano's fallboard and gone to bed.

There had still been no sign of the men today. They'd missed all their meals in the dining room, including this evening's sumptuous buffet.

A breeze carried a burst of laughter from the tent glowing bright against the black of the ocean. A crowd was gathered around a campfire singing and waiting for the moment when the lights the men had labored over would blink on in a brilliant display.

Fine icy crystals peppered Talia's face. She tucked her chin deeper into her scarf remembering yesterday's tree expedition. Here it was, a full day after Simao's declaration that he wanted Ethan to be his father, and the idea still caused her heart to jump.

They enjoyed each other's company. She even dared to think Ethan cared about her. But marriage? An instant family? He found great satisfaction in his work with the Agency, and her life was centered in New York City.

Her sigh turned frosty white in the cold air. Her thoughts were way ahead of the situation. She should be thinking about rearranging her apartment and life in the city to accommodate two children. Nearing the end of the boardwalk, she scanned the crowd and her heart tripped. The campfire silhouetted several broad-shouldered men.

The agents were no longer sequestered with Sam.

One broke away from the crowd.

Ethan. His smile sent a trill fluttering along her nerves. In an instant, the gloom that had held her captive lifted, and the stars overhead twinkled a little brighter.

"I'm sorry we missed last night." His melodious drawl was sweet music to her heart.

"Aggie said your disappearance was business as usual." The serious set of his features sent a riff of concern through her. "Is everything okay?"

"I have an hour, maybe two, before shipping out."

Her heart fell into her fur-lined boots. Knowing better than to ask him where he was going she asked the other, more important question. "When will you return?"

"I'm praying I'll be here for Christmas."

She turned and faced the campfire determined to hide the disappointment twisting through her. Soft strains of a guitar danced on the wind. "Who's playing?"

"Whit." Ethan shifted his stance. Below his knit cap, the moon dusted his cheeks with silvery light.

"Are any of the others going with you?"

"Depends on what Charlie works out. The St. John brothers for sure." Taking her hand, he pulled her into the tent. Platters of cookies were set out on tables. Behind a giant punchbowl, Aggie dispensed wassail mixed from her own secret recipe. He handed a thick paper cup to Talia.

She breathed in the steam and sipped the hot liquid. It carried a spicy kick and immediately began to melt the cold lump in the pit of her stomach.

He didn't take a cup for himself. "Sam entertains the neighbors to keep rumors and speculation at bay."

"What rumors?"

"Oh, you know. Regular stuff like we're a secret organization out to take over the world."

She couldn't detect even the smallest hint of a smile. "Are you serious?"

"Then there's the one about us being a cult."

She stared at him, unsure if he teased her.

Aggie clucked her tongue. "Don't you be telling tales and scaring the girl off. No sense at all. You shouldn't even be in here."

Surprise jolted through Talia. "Why?" His smile split her heart wide open.

"In her own bossy way, Aggie is suggesting I take you someplace a little more private." He waggled his eyebrows.

"Oh!" Warm wassail slopped over the rim of the cup soaking Talia's mitten.

He caught the cup as it slipped from her hand.

Aggie waved her ladle at him. "Was thinkin' no such thing! If you're leavin' to go who knows where, Sam won't want you near my wassail bowl."

Ethan leaned down and whispered, "In case you haven't noticed, the fumes alone could peel wallpaper."

Talia giggled, relishing the attention and the delicious shivers coursing through her.

A rousing chorus of "Jingle Bells" arose from the crowd around the campfire.

Setting her cup on the table, Ethan placed his hand at the small of her back and guided her to where Simao and Angelina stood off to one side listening. Their somber faces plucked at her overworked heartstrings.

"Come, children." She sat on a huge log before the fire and lifted Angelina onto her lap. Simao sat with his hands clasped between his knees. Ethan squeezed onto the end of the log on her other side.

Resting her chin beside the white pom pom on Angelina's hat, Talia stared at the flickering flames. *Lord, help me.* The prayer sifted through the fear and tender longings resonating in her heart.

A St. John brother handed Ethan a stick stacked with toasted marshmallows. Graham crackers and chocolate bars followed. Ethan assembled s'mores and handed one to each of the children.

Soon crumbs dusted the front of her niece's coat, and a sticky marshmallow string clung to her chin. Simao licked melted chocolate from his fingers. The simple sweet brought a broad smile to his face.

A flash of fear galloped wild through Talia.

She knew nothing about raising children. Yes, she'd taught in the school, but her students went home at the end of the day. They were not her responsibility every hour of every day until adulthood. Taking a deep breath, she closed her eyes and let the Christmas melody flow through her. *Father, help me to be a wise and discerning guardian.*

Chapter 14

Ethan couldn't keep his eyes off the woman sitting at his side. The fire touched her skin with its golden light, enhancing her profile. Her eyes were closed giving him an opportunity to study her smooth skin, winged eyebrows, and lush lips. He wasn't a man given to fanciful thoughts, but a halo seemed to glow in the curls framing her face. The thought of leaving her created an aching heaviness in his chest.

Last night, Sam called the team together for a video briefing. A security group responsible for the safety of an offshore oil field in the Gulf of Mexico had obtained intelligence on a credible threat to their installations. They were contacting SeaMount in the event they required mission support. Through the late night the decision makers in the Gulf ran through their options and the skills they needed from the SeaMount agents. Finally a decision was made, and the mission was a go.

A whistle pierced the crisp air, and the crowd quieted. Caleb Fallon stood at the end of the boardwalk dressed in a tuxedo. His fur-lined overcoat flapped in the ocean breeze. His fedora, cocked to one side, gave him the air of an old time movie star.

Ethan held out his hands to take Angelina, but Talia

shook her head. She let him help her to her feet instead.

"Friends and neighbors." Caleb's smooth baritone voice carried across the crowd. He held his wassail cup high, and in a dramatic, almost Shakespearean voice intoned, "Be joyful. Be merry. One and all now draw near. With music and lights, Christmas is here."

From high res speakers mounted on either side of the boardwalk, lively classical music filled the night air. In perfect synchronization, rows of fountain fireworks lit the sloping sand dune and lawn. Colorful pinwheels whirled on cue. The crowd exclaimed and clapped as row after crackling row of ground fireworks brightened the night, lighting the way to the looming building.

The last row of fountains threw sparks of green, red, silver, and gold into the air. The music hit its crescendo, and to the delight of the exuberant crowd, the lights on the bottom floor of the building flashed bright. Floor after floor, the lights winked on, gilding the huge Victorian building with golden brilliance.

Simao jumped and danced in the sand. He grabbed Ethan around the middle and squeezed.

Angelina lurched from Talia's arms and clutched Ethan's coat collar. He flung his arm out to catch her.

"Oh." Off balance, Talia stumbled against him grasping his jacket.

Throwing his other arm around her, he pulled her close. Standing in the center of the four-way hug, warmth flooded his chest and his breath hitched in the back of his throat. Talia's wide-eyed gaze held his for a long heart-stopping moment before Angelina wiggled and whined to be set down in the sand.

Talia's smile beamed bright in the lights reflected in her eyes. "That is beautiful."

You are beautiful. Her long lashes. The gentle curl of her ear. The slope of her nose. The tooth that overlapped its neighbor by a fraction. Ethan memorized her face, cataloging each detail, to be remembered on a lonely night in a country faraway.

"Hey, Squirt!"

The moment shattered as Davie burst on the scene, all teenage hormones and energy. He pulled Simao into a headlock. "Aggie has gingerbread men for us to decorate. Bet I can eat more than you."

Hanna's older sisters, Andi and Lissa Kerr, followed on his heels adding their voices to the invitation.

Knowing his goodbye couldn't wait, Ethan squatted on his heels and clasped Simao's hand. "I have to leave on assignment." For one fleeting memory, it was Josh standing in front of him trying to be brave. Ethan's heart cracked. "Promise to watch over your aunt and sister while I'm gone?"

Simao solemnly straightened his shoulders. "I will."

"Good man. Give me a hug."

Simao threw himself at Ethan and held on.

Ethan returned the hug then watched him race away with Davie and the girls.

"He has friends here." Talia's troubled look followed the children.

"You don't sound pleased."

"He'll have to say goodbye to them when we return to the city."

Her words ripped through him. The muscles in his shoulders tightened painfully. The thought of her leaving and taking the children with her overshadowed any relief he experienced knowing she'd made a decision. He yearned to talk to her—alone.

Sophie approached with Hanna. As if reading his mind, she pointed at Angelina. "I'll take her. We'll be in the tent decorating gingerbread men." She smiled at Talia. "Come join us when you're ready."

Ethan watched her go. "Did I miss something?" Talia's soft smile ramped his pulse into overdrive.

"Earlier tonight she offered to watch the children if you showed up."

Hand in hand they plodded across the soft sand away from the crowd and the lights. Overhead, stars sparkled in the wide onyx sky. The constant hiss and rumble of waves tumbling ashore filled the night. The thunder of the ocean echoed the pounding of Ethan's heart. "I have something to tell you, but I don't want to frighten you away."

She stiffened. In the ambient light, her eyes glittered. "I faced a student wielding a knife. I don't scare easy."

"Don't remind me. If I hadn't been there…."

"But you were." She squeezed his hand. "There are no coincidences."

For her to understand, he had to share his heart and soul. Sweat trickled between his shoulder blades. He couldn't find the fancy words to ease into it, so he simply said it. "God speaks to me in dreams." It was blunt and to the point, and he didn't try to fill the silence that followed. She would puzzle through what he'd said, and believe him…or not.

"How long—?"

"Started in my teens." He looked out over the ocean, down at his feet. Any place but at her.

She stepped in front of him to get his attention. "What does He show you?" Dismay swept across her face. "The accident." Her voice dropped to a whisper. "Did you have foreknowledge of your wife and son's death?"

He pulled her into his arms to silence her. "No." The

denial came out a low growl. "God doesn't give me more than I can handle." *Thank you, Jesus.*

Her question opened a Pandora's box of memories, but only two mattered in this conversation.

"After their death, I kept dreaming of Joshua." His chest ached. He pulled in a shaky breath. "He was so happy. Felt so close. I welcomed those dreams. I relived them every waking hour. I climbed into bed at night hoping Josh would be waiting for me in my dreams." Even now he wanted to lose himself in the remembering. "After several months the oddest thing happened." *She'll think I'm crazy.* "Josh's face faded, and I'd see another boy's face." He tightened his arms, unwilling to let go if she tried to escape his grasp. "That boy was Simao."

To his relief, she didn't pull away. Instead she leaned closer and wrapped her arms around him. "The first time you saw Simao...."

"Was on St. Beatrice."

"Oh." Her body jerked. "Were you shocked?" Her voice trembled.

"Yes." And the shock hadn't ended with the appearance of Simao.

Tell her.

The sand shifted beneath his boots. "There's more." His throat tightened painfully.

Face upturned, she watched him.

Just say the words, Thomas. "Lacey—my wife—when she died...she was pregnant with...our daughter." His voice choked off.

Around his waist, Talia's arms tightened.

He looked up and searched the heavens as he had so many times since that fateful night. The stars blurred. He'd begun, and he had to finish. "We hadn't told anyone. We treasured the secret. We couldn't agree on a name for her so...." His voice wobbled. *Get a grip, man.* "I called her 'Angel.'" He pulled in air like a drowning man. "She was my little angel."

Talia gasped. "Angelina!"

"Yeah." He exhaled the word. "Crazy the way God works."

She stared at him in silence, and his heart faltered. It dropped to his toes when she withdrew her arms from around him. But then her mittens skimmed over his chest and across his collar to cradle his cheeks.

"I...." She paused, searching for words. "You've wrapped your mind around this, Ethan." Her gaze brushed across his face in puzzlement. "I'm still trying to understand." She hesitated. "God's ways are mysterious, and I will never have all the answers, but I have to think this through as much as I'm able." Her brow crinkled. "Okay?"

Drowning in her solemn look, he didn't pull away. He pressed his brow to hers and let himself sink into the warm depth of her eyes. "However long it takes." Her tremulous smile caused his heart to kick.

Her hands slipped from his face, and she rested her cheek against his chest.

Ethan lost track of time as they stood in a quiet embrace. He hoped and prayed what he'd revealed wouldn't send her running.

In his pocket, his phone vibrated. "Walk with me to the car."

"You have to go now?"

"Yes." He led her across the sand and the lawn to the path that led to the parking lot.

She slowed and looked at him. A million questions flashed in her eyes.

He pulled her close and hushed her with a kiss. Her scent, a heady combination of mandarin orange and spice, swirled around him. She squeaked, and he loosened his grip.

She breathed deeply of the salt air.

"You okay?" His fingers worried the edge of her scarf.

She nodded. "Just…needed…air."

He rubbed his cheek against her soft hair and murmured, "Poor lung capacity."

Nearby a car engine turned over. The St. John brothers jogged past. They grinned and tossed him a thumbs-up.

Ethan's heart thudded slow. If he'd had any doubts about his feelings for Talia, this goodbye had squashed them. He wanted her in his life. And he shouldn't. *He wasn't ready for this…was he?*

Talia patted his chest with her mitten-covered hand. "You take care of yourself, you hear me, Ethan Thomas?"

"Yes, ma'am." Her lighthearted attempt endeared her to him all the more.

"Good. Go do what you have to do, and come home in time for Christmas."

It was best not to make promises he may not be able to keep. Ethan let another kiss speak for him before jogging to the black SUV. Leaving the parking lot, he allowed himself one glance back.

She stood alone in the brilliant wash of light created by the thousands of bulbs trimming the building he called home.

Chapter 15

Standing at the window of her high-rise apartment, Talia looked out over the panoramic night view of Lower Manhattan. She'd never realized how the glow of city lights dulled the night sky. There were very few stars compared to the hundreds she'd seen in the heavens while on the beach with Ethan. *What is he doing? Is he safe?* Christmas was only three days away. Would he make it home for the holiday?

Plucking a pink kitten off the rug, she tucked it into bed beside Angelina. The sleeping child was a tiny bump in her queen size bed.

Ethan had been gone nine days. Not a one had passed that she didn't think about all that he'd revealed the night of the open house. What he shared was incredible. What she kept coming back to was how little she understood God and the mystery of His ways. Why did Ethan have to suffer the loss of his family? Why bring her niece and nephew into his life?

And you! Like the rumble of the lowest note on the piano keyboard, the voice vibrated through her.

Me? It's like you're giving him a replacement family, Lord. I won't be a substitute wife. Second best was not a role she could embrace. Not that the man had proposed marriage to her. But, what if he did? Her heart fluttered. Did she love him?

Surprise rippled through her. *Why wasn't her first thought about her career as a teacher?*

"Aunt Tallie?" Simao stood at the bedroom door dressed in Ninja pajamas. "I'm hungry."

She left the bedroom, relieved to put an end to the soul-searching. "I have graham crackers in the cupboard." Earlier, he'd devoured a burger at the deli across the street. She didn't believe the problem was hunger, but she couldn't be sure.

Would she *ever* be sure about *anything* when it came to mothering her sister's children? "Sit here." At the dinette table, she set out a glass of milk and a plate of crackers. She took the seat across from him.

His lack of interest in the food confirmed her suspicions.

"What's wrong, Simao?" *Lord, give me the ability to handle the problem.*

After a few moments hesitation, he blurted out, "I miss Ethan."

"Me, too." When Simao asked about his grandfather, she'd jumped at the opportunity to come to the city for a visit. She'd hoped seeing Papa would pull her out of the endless pining for Ethan. A sigh escaped her lips. *Well, a girl could hope.*

"Will he come home for Christmas?"

"I hope so. I pray everyday for his safe return. Just remember, he's doing a job he loves, and we can be proud of him." *Are you listening to yourself, Talia?*

Simao nibbled at his graham cracker. His gaze traveled around the combined living room and kitchen finally stopping at the painting hanging beside the front door—a print of Horace Pippin's *Man on a Bench*. "Who is that man?"

One of her students had given her the print as a gift. She adored it. The man relaxing on the bench reminded her of Papa when he was much younger. "I don't know who the artist used for the model. He painted the picture many, many years ago."

Simao's pensive gaze continued past the chocolate brown sofa where vibrant red and yellow pillows added color. A red floor vase filled with silk flowers stood to the right of the cherry entertainment center.

Talia ran her fingers through her hair. Her bracelets chimed softly. Was he comparing her home to SeaMount? Her home was small. *Too small to raise two children.* Her heart pinged. She loved the home she'd created, but for the first time ever, she was restless in these four walls.

Simao scooted off his chair and wrapped his arms around her neck. "Thank you for bringing us here."

She returned the hug, grateful he was starting to trust that life could be good again. "Now, off to bed. Tomorrow's a big day. You'll meet your grandpapa."

He ran to the sofa, which Talia had made into a bed.

Drawing the blanket up to his chin, she kissed his cheek. "No matter what happens you and Angelina have a home."

He smiled and snuggled deeper into the cushions. "Ethan said the same thing."

Talia's heart bumped hard. *What had prompted Ethan's declaration?*

"Grandpapa." Simao held the knobby hand that hung slack from the arm of the wheelchair.

Papa's eyes followed Angelina as she climbed onto his bed and made herself comfortable.

Talia lifted his sax from its battered case. "Play for us, Papa." Over breakfast, she'd explained to the children how her father no longer remembered the life he'd lived. *There was so much she would never know about her mother and sister.* A shard of anger pierced her heart. She'd fought the battle to forgive many times over the past several weeks. Each time it became a little easier to give her hurt to God.

She kissed his cheek and handed him the instrument, once again reminding herself he was the only father she'd ever have.

He ran his fingertips over the ligature screws.

Talia opened the reed case and selected one for him. As a professional musician he'd been ritualistic about preparing his reeds. No longer capable of performing that task, she'd bought him this case to keep them at the proper humidity.

His fingers fumbled through what, at one time, had been second nature. He lifted the mouthpiece to his lips and one by one, six notes swelled and filled the room. The tone he created was no longer the best, but the children didn't know or care. They danced to their grandfather's music and filled the room with their happiness.

Simao tugged on the sleeve of Talia's sweater. "The Christmas present, Aunt Tallie."

She pulled a brightly wrapped package from the tote at her feet. "Here you go."

"Merry Christmas, Grandpapa." Simao placed the gift on his grandfather's thin knees clad in blue sweatpants. Angelina bounced with excitement.

Her father set his instrument aside. He enjoyed receiving gifts. The loss of his memory had not dimmed the pleasure he found in colorful paper and ribbons. He plucked at the bow and ran his hand over the glossy paper.

"You may help him unwrap it."

Simao pulled the bow off and unstuck the tape, all the while talking to his grandfather.

Talia snapped photos on her cell phone wishing again she'd known the women—her sister and mother—who had raised the children to be so caring.

Holding the children's homemade card, Papa touched the cotton ball snowman. Simao read the sentiment he'd painstakingly printed. On some level, the love in the message reached through the veil that cast its heavy shadow over Papa's mind. He patted Simao's shoulder and ran his hand over Angelina's soft curls.

Helping his grandfather tear away the paper, Simao held up the blue sweater they'd bought. "See, Grandpapa? There is a tag with your name on it." The facility's requirement that the resident's name be on every article of clothing intrigued him.

A chime played announcing dinner. Having made previous arrangements, they accompanied Papa to the dining hall. The children received the attention of the elderly crowd with a composure that pleased Talia. While they finished the last of their pudding, and Papa dozed in his chair, she watched the television mounted high on the wall.

A closed-captioned weather forecast with radar filled the screen. The winter storm originally predicted to stay at sea now skirted the mainland. High winds and snow were expected to cause havoc with holiday travel.

Unsettled, Talia wheeled Papa to his room. The children lingered over their goodbyes. Talia cupped his wrinkled face in her hands and kissed his brow. "Merry Christmas, Papa."

She filled the final awkward moments of leaving with the zipping of zippers, donning hats, and finding mittens.

They stepped out of the facility's warm cocoon and into an icy blast. Large snowflakes plopped on every surface, mottling the world with fluffy crystals. Giggling, the children tried to catch the mammoth flakes on their tongues.

"Come along." Talia shivered. She had planned one more night in the city before leaving very early tomorrow—Christmas Eve. But the forecast was threatening. Heavy gray clouds already hid the tops of the tallest buildings. They needed to leave today. If Ethan made it home for Christmas, she wanted to be there.

The rhythmic sway of the passenger car and the clack of the rails lulled the children to sleep. Thankful to have three seats together on the crowded train, Talia stared out the window. Between the early dusk of winter and the near whiteout conditions, she couldn't see anything beyond her own reflection.

She'd called Charlie earlier to tell him what time their train would arrive at the station. In less than two hours they'd be home. A happy zing rippled through her. *Home?* Her home was here in the city.

But your heart is in Rhode Island.

She couldn't deny the soul deep whisper. SeaMount had become a part of her. The people there were as close as family and cared for each other. One man in particular held her heart in his big hands, and if he wanted it, her future, as well. She sighed. *Lord, show me your will. Ethan... Papa... The children. I love them all.*

Taking her cell phone from her purse, she scrolled through the photos she'd taken of the children with Papa. Selecting the best one, she sent it to Ethan with a short message. "*On r way home. C u soon?*" That done she rested her head against the seat and closed her eyes.

She awoke to a screeching roar that had its origin in Hades. Talia's seat shook and rocked. She clutched the armrests. Her heart leapt into her throat, and her mouth dried cottony.

Angelina awoke with a scream.

Talia reached for her niece, but before she could get a hold on her, an unseen force lifted Angelina and flung her over the seats. A scream clawed at Talia's throat. She slammed against the seat in front of her then was whipped to one side. Something heavy landed on her, forcing the air from her lungs. Pain exploded in her head and the cries around her faded to nothing.

Chapter 16

Under bright floodlights, Ethan and the St. John brothers stowed their gear in the rental car Charlie had reserved for them. One travel delay after another had come their way—the final delay being the snowstorm that clung to the east coast. Their flight had been rerouted from T. F. Green Airport in Rhode Island to Bradley International in Windsor Locks, Connecticut.

Ethan climbed behind the wheel of the SUV. Phones glowing, Gabe and Logan monitored weather alerts and road closings. Thankfully, they hadn't seen so much as one snowflake—yet.

"Doesn't look good."

That ominous statement from the backseat set Ethan's teeth on edge. Talia had sent him a picture and text saying they were on their way home. For ten days—he'd counted every one—she and the children had filled his thoughts. Tomorrow was only a few hours away. A snowstorm was not going to stop him from getting home for Christmas Eve. Wanting a distraction, he punched the radio button and tuned into an all news station.

"Breaking news." The radio announcer's voice filled the interior of the vehicle. *"We've received a report of a*

derailment of a northbound train. The accident occurred outside of Guilford, Connecticut."

Like a hot electrical current, a frisson of worry raced through him.

Gabe tapped furiously on the screen of his phone as the announcer continued to speak.

"The train was meant to switch to a different track. But due to snow covering the signal, the crew missed the warning to slow down on the approach to the crossover. The heavy snow is now hampering rescue measures. The injured are being transported to local hospitals. So far, we know of two fatalities."

"What train are they on?" The light from his phone's LCD screen etched Gabe's features into sharp angles.

Ethan jabbed the radio's on/off button. "Can't be their train. Can't be." The phone in his pocket buzzed, and his heart dropped into his damp boots. He dug it out and glanced at the display. *Sam.*

He hit the hands-free speaker button. "Yeah?" His voice rasped.

"Where are you?"

He bit out their location before asking the question uppermost in his mind. "Is Talia home?" The pause that followed sent his heart into overdrive.

"Listen to me, Thomas." Sam's no-nonsense voice jerked Ethan away from the brink of panic.

"Yes, sir."

"There's been an accident."

The past flashed through his mind, and pain ripped through his solar plexus. *He was home. A police officer stood at the door. "There's been an accident."* Panic burned in his chest. He spoke over whatever Sam was saying. "Were they on the train that derailed?"

"Yes."

The control that served him so well in his job abandoned him. The phone slipped from his shaking hand, and Gabe caught it.

Ethan tried to picture the scene. His imagination flew in all directions. They were fine. They were not in the cars that derailed. Then the movies in his head flipped, placing Talia and the children smack in the middle of the most horrific disaster he'd witnessed. Fighting for control, he pulled air into his lungs determined to regulate his breathing. He'd be no good to anyone if he couldn't think straight.

Gabe finished the conversation with the director. "We're to head toward the accident. In the meantime, he and Charlie will work the phones to locate Talia and the kids."

"Watch for the next exit." In the backseat, Logan stared at his phone. "We'll be on secondary roads. Snow will cause a problem, but it's a more direct route."

Neither man asked Ethan to give up the wheel. He would have flat out refused. He had to be doing something, and right now the only thing he could do was drive.

Less than five miles from the accident they ran into the storm.

A smattering of snowflakes flew at them in the brightly lit tunnel created by the SUV's low beams. Then, an icy white curtain fell and swirled around the vehicle.

Headlights reflected off the heavy wet snow, slowing their progress to a crawl. Twice they stopped to clear it from the sides of the windshield where the wipers had packed it into frozen ridges.

After what felt like an eternity, Ethan spied a flashing light ahead. A huge dump truck plowing the snow took a left turn. Logan confirmed it was headed the direction they wanted to go. Ethan followed.

They traveled another slow mile before reaching the outskirts of town. The hazy lights of homes and businesses glowed yellow through the thick veil of snow. They saw several snowplows working as teams to clear and sand the road.

The scream of a siren broke the silence. Lights flashed across the crystalline landscape.

An ambulance emerged from a side road that was partially blocked by a police car. Ethan pulled over on the shoulder as far as the snow allowed to let the emergency vehicle pass.

On a hunch he turned to take that side road. The SUV's headlights reflected off the orange safety vest of a police officer stepping from his cruiser.

Ethan lowered his window. Snow blew in, dusting his face and shoulders.

The officer's eyes skated over the three men. "This is a restricted area."

"Yes, sir." Ethan struggled to remain calm. "We're from the SeaMount Agency. Here to help with the rescue effort." Though not invited to participate, it was still a fact. They were there, and they could help.

The officer shook his head, not buying it. "Only authorized personnel allowed beyond this point."

Ethan stared straight ahead. He couldn't leave. Not when he was this close.

In the backseat, Logan's phone buzzed. He muttered and leaned forward between the seats. "Thanks, officer. You take care." He pressed a fist to Ethan's shoulder. "Let's go."

In the rearview mirror, Ethan nailed him with a glare. He would not give up so easily.

Logan waved his phone in the air.

The call. Ethan shifted the SUV in gear and slowly pulled away.

"The local hospital is the triage center." Logan's thumbs flew as he typed in the address. "Sam wants us to head there while he sorts through red tape."

Please, Lord, let them be alive. Negotiating a hill, Ethan held the steering wheel in a death grip. The road that had just been plowed and sanded was already blanketed in white.

Through the bare tree trunks in the valley to their right, emergency floodlights shined and glinted off the steel exterior of a train's passenger cars. No longer on the rails in a neat straight line, they rested in haphazard disarray. Rescue workers scurried to and fro like neon-vested ants.

"Why're you slowing down?" Gabe's eyes narrowed. "Don't do this, Thomas. Go to the hospital."

Ethan's need to be on the scene was overwhelming. *Talia and the children.* He had to find them. He stopped the SUV. His hand groped for the door handle.

"No." Gabe dove across the console.

Ethan ducked from the vehicle, Gabe's grabbing hands nothing but an annoyance. He skirted around the rear bumper. The brothers were waiting for him.

He plowed through them slipping and sliding down the hill. Brush slapped and snatched at his clothing. A switch sliced across his cheek. *"Oof."* Rammed hard from behind, he fell face first in the snow.

The brothers were on him, wrestling to hold him. "Sam said the hospital.... No good to Talia...or the kids...like this."

He rose on all fours, and a trickle of cold snow slid beneath his collar.

They grappled with him, battling for the upper hand.

One brother grunted. "Can't get his arm 'round behind…too stinkin' big."

The other breathed close to Ethan's ear. "Don't make me knock you out."

"You carryin' 'im to the car, bro?"

"Listen to us, you big lummox." Gabe shook the scruff of Ethan's collar. "She may not even be here. She could be on her way to the hospital."

On his knees, Ethan stopped struggling. He sucked in biting cold air as fear wedged razor sharp in his chest. All around him the snow blew. It swept through the low brush creating a frozen canvas. From the shifting play of light and shadow there emerged a picture. His breath rasped in his throat. *Talia.* Lying among bits of clothing and other debris. Her eyes were closed as though sleeping.

"No." He struggled to his feet. With the strength of a man gone mad, he fought off his snarling teammates. They were big, and they were strong, but desperation added fuel to his already considerable strength.

"You're a blasted giant—*ooph!*"

A well-placed elbow caused one pair of hands to fall away. By the time Ethan reached the bottom of the hill, he'd left the other brother behind as well. He charged through the thinning trees and burst into the open stopping only to get his bearings in the disaster's organized chaos.

He'd been a part of operations like this one more times than he cared to count. Rescue vehicles and ambulances waited on the ballast apron as first responders cared for casualties.

Three passenger cars had jumped the rails, slid down the track bed, and tumbled onto their sides. Fire trucks were supplying ladders to access the cars and ease the evacuation of victims.

Ethan stumbled toward the closest one. Rescuers were at the top of a ladder lifting a litter through the narrow opening of the crumpled door. A glimpse of the bloodied face confirmed the casualty was not Talia or either of the children.

God, help me. Lending a hand at the bottom of the ladder, he waited for an opening to climb up. Behind him, Gabe and Logan ran interference with an official. Scaling the ladder he lowered himself into the car. The vestibule had absorbed most of the crushing force as the cars rammed into each other.

Ducking low, he entered the car finding footing on the side of a seat. A jumble of luggage, debris, and bloody clothing buried the side of the car and its shattered windows.

He spotted an exposed arm here, a stockinged foot there. Calling on every bit of reserve he had, he mentally picked apart the tangle of clothing finding the shapes of bodies stacked, in some places, three deep.

Overhead, boots dangled through the emergency exit window. Logan dropped in next to him. "Take these. Biggest they got." He held out a fistful of blue nitrile gloves.

The sight of them yanked Ethan from his bubble of misery and set him into motion. He pulled on a pair and climbed into the thick of the confusion. The acrid odor of blood and body fluids hung heavy in the close quarters.

He worked alongside Logan and the other rescuers administering first aid. He worked by rote, trying to keep his mind focused on the person in front of him. The need to find Talia soon propelled him to the door as the injured were evacuated.

Stationing himself at the bent doorframe, he lent his muscle to lifting the litters. He'd seen all the injured in *this* railcar. Grateful for that much, he chafed to go through the other cars.

Logan approached from the other end of the car, stepping past the last of the injured being prepped for evacuation.

His teammate's expression made Ethan pause. "Talia?" He glanced back. *Had he missed her?*

Logan shook his head. "Not here. Gabe…." He motioned for Ethan to climb out.

Heart thundering to life, Ethan tossed aside his soiled gloves and followed Logan. He jumped to the ground and landed with a thud. Snow continued to fall, covering the scene of horror in pristine white. "Where is she?"

Logan paused and tipped his head to one side as if listening.

Ready to leap out of his skin, Ethan waited. The identical twin brothers possessed an uncanny bond. Clearer and stronger when one needed the other, what tied them together defied scientific explanation.

"This way." Logan sprinted to the cars that were derailed but hadn't tipped over. He stopped at a car with one end on the rail and the other end rammed against an outcropping of granite. "This one." Grasping the handrail, he jumped onto the twisted stairs and disappeared inside.

Ethan followed and scrutinized the length of the car, heart thudding with hope. He forced his way up the aisle to where Gabe tended a crying child.

"*Angelina!*" Thinking with his heart instead of his head, he picked her up thanking God she had the ability to wail so loud.

"Nothing broken. Cut on her arm. Mostly banged up."

Ethan barely heard Gabe's assessment of Angelina's injuries over the adrenaline roaring through him.

"I have Simao."

Turning toward Logan's voice, Ethan took a direct hit as the boy lunged. Dropping into the nearest seat, he held both of them tight. They had suffered only superficial wounds. A miracle compared to what he'd seen in the rolled cars.

Logan's voice carried over the crying. "They're small and would have been thrown farther."

The brothers exchanged a look.

Gabe peeled the kids off of Ethan. "Go. I'll stay with these two."

Unable to stop the trembling in his arms and legs, Ethan rose to search with Logan. Wading through debris, he checked under seats and beneath jumbled luggage.

Three rows away, a first responder in an orange vest bent over someone hidden between the rows of seats.

"My children."

The words punched the air from Ethan's lungs. *"Talia."* He muscled his way past the man, ignoring the angry words aimed at him. The need to hold her was as irrepressible as the reflex to draw his next breath.

"Ethan?" Relief laced her voice, but her eyes remained dark with fear. "Where are they?"

"Gabe has them." Stroking her soft curls, his fingers came away sticky with blood. "Don't move." Using the sterile dressing someone handed him, he pressed it against the wound above her ear.

A dewy sheen of sweat covered her brow. Above her knee, blood soaked a gaping rip in her slacks.

Logan climbed over the seats to help the EMT work on Talia's leg.

Ethan cupped her head in his hands. "Look at me, Talia. The kids are banged up but fine." Gazing into her pain filled eyes, it was all he could do to hold himself together. With shaking hands, he wrapped her head with gauze.

They strapped her to a litter. Outside the rail car he helped transfer her to a waiting stretcher. Gabe approached with the children, and Ethan wrapped an arm around Simao's shoulders. "Talk to your aunt, buddy. Let her hear your voice."

Simao leaned close and whispered something in her ear. Whatever the kid said made her lips twitch into a brief smile. It wasn't much, but it was enough for Ethan.

Chapter 17

From the passenger van's last row of seats, Talia looked out the window. The meds the hospital had given her for pain had also made her sleepy. Snuggled close to Ethan, she'd dozed some of the way home. She sighed, and he dropped a light kiss on the top of her head. Her floaty feeling wasn't entirely due to the pain meds.

The winter storm had ended early this morning. As soon as travel bans were lifted in three states, Sam had arranged for this luxury van and driver to bring everyone home. He'd even remembered to include a child's safety seat for Angelina.

Ethan hadn't left her side at the hospital. Something about him had changed. Perhaps the accident had brought him face to face with the same revelation she'd experienced. God had brought them together for a purpose. There was a bigger plan playing out, and she didn't need to fear what was going to happen—between them, with Papa, or with her career.

The van ascended the narrow road leading to the top of the bluff overlooking the ocean. She was eager to see the twinkling lights rimming the SeaMount building. Her gaze tangled with Ethan's, and her heart thrummed. Could she truly feel at home here?

"What are you thinking?" The words rumbled deep in his chest.

"I'm anxious to get the children settled." As fibs went it wasn't the most brilliant.

A smile played across his wide mouth. "Don't be disappointed if that doesn't happen right away."

"Why?"

He nuzzled her ear and whispered, "It's Christmas Eve, Tallie. We have traditions." He kissed her, sending delicious shivers racing down her neck and across her shoulders.

The van pulled into the half circle drive and stopped behind the lit nativity. The building sparkled like something straight out of a Christmas movie.

"Here we are." Ethan gently shook the sleeping children. "Wake up. We're home."

Home. Hearing him say that word warmed her deep inside. *One step at a time. Lord, open my heart to your plan.*

The van stopped, and the side door slid open. Whit poked his head in, a grin on his face. "Welcome home."

Talia smiled back. *Yes. Home.* More and more, she liked the sound of that.

Whit lifted a sleepy Angelina from her seat. Simao climbed out in slow motion. He didn't fuss when Logan picked him up and carried him indoors.

Before Talia realized his intent, Ethan slipped his arms around her and lifted her from the vehicle. She squeaked with surprise. "They gave me crutches."

He swung around to mount the steps. "If you're in my arms I know you're not getting into trouble." He paused, a mischievous glint in his dark eyes. "Well, trouble I can't handle."

His words, softly spoken in his melodious voice, swirled

through her, melting the last remnants of fear and distress she'd suffered in the accident. He carried her into the sitting room where flames popped and crackled in the fireplace.

With gentle care, he placed her on the sofa and unbuttoned her coat.

Dressed in garish Christmas sweaters, Charlie and Caleb greeted her and the children with enthusiasm.

"You're home!" Aggie bustled into the room followed by Sophie.

Aggie's choice of words tickled Talia. "Yes, we're home." Ethan helped her slip out of her coat. The hospital had given her green scrubs to replace the slacks they'd cut off in the emergency room.

Aggie eyed them and asked, "How do you feel? You in pain?"

"Tired and kind of dopey. They gave me good drugs."

Sophie rested a hand on Talia's shoulder. "We're having a light supper before attending the early Christmas Eve service. If you'd rather not go, I can stay here with you."

"Thank you, but I want to go." God had protected her and the children from great harm. She wanted to be in His house to praise Him and thank Him.

Sophie gently squeezed her shoulder. "Then let's go up to your suite so you can freshen up."

Gray entered the room pushing a wheelchair, and Ethan lifted Talia into it.

Sophie collected Talia's coat. "Angelina and Simao, why don't you join our girls and Davie in the dining room for cocoa and cookies."

"Spoiling their supper." Gray's muttering earned him a gentle poke in the ribs.

"It's Christmas Eve. Don't be a Scrooge." Sophie's impertinent reprimand earned her a tender whack on the bottom and a lingering kiss before Gray joined the men in front of the fire.

Ethan pushed Talia onto the elevator and rode up to the guest rooms. Entering her suite, he set the brake on the chair. "I'll stay."

Sophie placed a hand on his arm. "I'll help Talia."

"Doctor said to keep the dressings dry."

"I promise they'll stay dry."

"She might fall in the bathroom."

"We'll be careful she doesn't."

He dropped onto the sofa and settled back. "Then go do what you have to do."

Sophie plunked her hands on her hips.

Uh-oh. Talia's hands tightened on the arms of the chair. If she didn't intervene the argument would go on without resolution. "Ethan."

He sprang up. "What?"

She cupped his cheek with her hand and kissed him. "This is our first Christmas Eve together." Her tummy twanged. She wanted more than just this one. "I want a picture of us with the children and, well, you look like you've been in a train wreck."

His anxious eyes crinkled at the corners. "Me?" He looked down. Blood, now the color of old brick, smeared his jacket. The knee of his pants gaped with a three cornered tear. "Oh."

"Go shower and change. Then come back and escort me to supper."

He hesitated, no doubt calculating the time it would take him to sprint to his room, shower, and return to her suite.

Sophie opened the door. "The sooner you leave, the sooner she'll be ready."

Eyes on Talia, Ethan backed out of the room.

Sophie closed the door in his face. A moment later, they heard running feet thunder down the hall.

The women grinned at each other and burst into laughter.

"We better get busy." Sophie wheeled Talia into the bedroom closing the door behind them. "If he's anything like Gray, he'll be back in less than ten minutes."

"Ten minutes! I won't be ready."

Sophie rolled Talia's chair through the bedroom and into the well-appointed bathroom. The mirror over the vanity reflected their images. "Then prepare to have a conversation through the closed door." Turning on the faucet, she filled the basin. "Every man here has a protective gene the size of North America. They're adamant about taking care of their own." She handed Talia a moist facecloth. "And don't deny it. Ethan believes you belong to him."

Heat sizzled through Talia, warming her cheeks. "He hasn't said anything specific."

"They're men of action first. The words come later."

Sophie's help with washing away the last vestiges of the accident lifted Talia's spirits. They were in the bedroom giggling as they debated the choice of a skirt or slacks when a fist banged on the hall door startling them.

"You ready?" Ethan's muffled question sent them into another fit of giggles.

"I didn't lock that door when I shut it in his face." Sophie set the slacks aside and held up the skirt. "This'll be faster."

Sitting on the edge of the bed, Talia called out to him. "That door isn't locked. Make yourself at home on the sofa." Sophie dropped the skirt over her head and shoulders. It puddled around her waist.

"Are you ready yet?" Ethan spoke close to the other side of the bedroom door.

"No."

"How long you gonna be?"

Sophie's eyes sparkled with laughter. Talia clapped her hand over her mouth to muffle the giggles strangling her.

"You okay in there? Can I help you?"

"No!" In unison Talia and Sophie yelled back.

"Okay. Okay." A rhythmic pacing began in the sitting room.

Talia discovered new places that hurt as Sophie helped her into a patchwork sweater decorated with Christmas motifs. Finding the battery box, she flipped the LED lights to blinking mode. The price of admission to the evening's celebration was a tacky Christmas sweater. "I'll switch this off before entering the church."

Sophie pulled a pair of red leather flats from the closet and knelt to slip them on Talia's feet.

The pacing stopped just outside the door. "What's taking so long in there?"

"I'm picking out my shoes."

"Why? You're not walking anywhere."

"They go with the outfit." Talia forced the words around the laughter rising in her throat.

"Your feet are swollen." Sophie's whisper brought Talia back to the problem at hand. Her groan prompted another question from the other side of the door.

"What's wrong?"

Sophie answered, "Ethan Thomas, unless you know more than we do about women's shoes, you have nothing to add to this conversation." In the silence that followed Sophie found Talia's soft, gold slippers. They slipped on easily. A bedspring squeaked as she transferred to the wheelchair.

"What are you doing?" On the other side of the door, Ethan rattled the knob.

"Hair and makeup are next. And the door is locked."

Sophie wheeled Talia into the bathroom and murmured, "Not that a locked door will stop him. Honestly! The bigger they are the harder they fall."

They worked fast and managed to fend off Ethan for another ten minutes before opening the door. The relief on his face was as comical as the reindeer with the red pompom nose that decorated the front of his sweater.

Talia fluffed her hair. "Was I worth the wait?" His heart-stopping smile sparked a flame deep inside her.

"Absolutely." He dropped to his knee and ran his finger along her jawline. "I'm near crazy worrying about you. I can't lose you, too."

He looked away, but not before she saw the haunting sadness deep in his eyes. Unwilling to let ghosts of the past ruin their evening, Talia gave his shoulder a gentle shake. "You haven't lost me. I'm right here, and I'm starving. Do I have time for a bite to eat before church?"

"You do." Rising, he rolled her chair through the hall door Sophie held open.

Talia soaked in the music sung by the robed choir. Red poinsettias rimmed the dais. Pine garlands wrapped each column filling the sanctuary with their tangy scent. Subdued candlelight flickered among the worshipers as a small flame was passed from one person to the next. Soon every hand-held candle in the sanctuary was lit. Under the watchful eyes of the St. John brothers, Simao and Angelina's faces glowed in the light of their small white candles.

Family. That was the other word that kept intruding on Talia's thoughts. With a home, comes a family. Sam and Aggie and the men of SeaMount were celebrating Christmas together as a family. Only Preach was not there. He'd flown to Kansas to spend the holiday with his fiancée. Charlie wasn't at the church service because he'd left on a mysterious errand. He'd assured everyone he'd be back in time to eat.

Talia closed her eyes and joined in singing the final carol of the service. Aggie's warble and Sam's gravelly bass blended with the mellow masculine harmony of the men. In the beauty of the moment, tears escaped and ran in gentle rivulets down her cheeks. Her shoulders quaked as she held back a sob. The carol ended, and she bowed her head.

"Tallie?" Ethan sank to his knees at her side. He blew out her candle before wrapping his arm around her shoulders. His brow rested warm against her temple. His moist breath feathered along her neck. "Is it your leg? Are you in pain?"

Trembling all over, she shook her head. "It's…just…everything…."

"Shhh." He pulled a handkerchief from his pocket and wiped her cheeks. She took it and cried until her throat burned raw. Her sister and mother were beyond her reach. She'd only just met Simao and Angelina. If she had lost them…. *Get a grip, Talia.* She squeezed her eyes together and dabbed them with the soggy handkerchief. Ethan's hand, warm and solid, rubbed a comforting circle between her shoulder blades.

She looked at him and tried to smile.

"You okay now?"

The furrows in his brow needed to be smoothed out, but she didn't trust her shaky hand to hit the mark. "Yes." His sigh of relief made her smile. "I've ruined my makeup."

"You're still beautiful." In the low lights his dark eyes held hers for a long electric moment. Unexpressed feelings flowed like a hot current between them.

"Let's go then." Pushing her through the crowd, he wheeled her down the handicap exit ramp, across the street, and up the portable ramp Sam had installed at the agency. Having used the ramp for the first time on the way to church, she was grateful for the gruff director's thoughtfulness.

Whit peeled away from the group standing on the front porch and opened the door for them. The man's devilish grin gave Talia a moment's pause, but Ethan didn't seem to notice, so she let it go and sat back to enjoy the evening.

Simao and Angelina knelt with Sophie's girls before the tree. Beneath the wide branches were giftwrapped boxes. There was one for each child, including Davie, who hovered between the men and the children, undecided where he belonged.

An air of expectancy swirled through the room surprising Talia with its intensity.

In the hall, the soft *ding* of the elevator bell signaled Charlie's return. But it wasn't his voice that greeted everyone with "Merry Christmas, dears."

Angelina and Simao squealed and raced across the room. They wrapped themselves around an older woman not much taller than Simao.

"My, how both of you have grown. Angelina, you are beautiful." The woman wore a red felt hat with a curling ostrich plume. She carried a huge purse. Charlie stood behind her holding a cat kennel.

"Ethan, who is she?" Talia watched Whit move in to sweep the woman into a bear hug.

"Let me introduce you." Ethan moved her chair closer. The men parted for her to pass. "Talia Combs meet Ava Endicott Smythe Fairfax Meriwether. Ava, this is Simao and Angelina's aunt."

"Oh my, yes." The woman hugged Talia. "The children are so fortunate to have you."

"You're Miss Ava?" Talia blinked hard and returned the hug. "Simao told me about their time with you. Thank you for watching over them."

A quiet *snick* was followed by a hair-raising yowl. An orange ball of fur leapt across Talia's lap. She screamed with surprise. The children shrieked, and the animal darted away. It raced into the dining room where there was a loud crash of plates breaking and silverware rattling.

The men looked at each other in horror before racing to the dining room.

A moment of shock followed before Simao said, "Angelina did it."

Angelina's bottom lip trembled.

Blocking out the shouts and thud of running boots, Talia held her hands out to Angelina. "Come here, sweetie." Talia hugged her. "Who did you let out of the kennel?"

"Puuumpkiiiin." Angelina wailed and knuckled her eyes.

Talia rubbed her back. "Next time, please let Miss Ava decide when and where to open the door. Okay?"

Angelina peeked at Miss Ava being escorted to the dining room by Whit. She nodded her head in exaggerated agreement.

Biting her lip to keep from smiling, Talia glanced at Ethan. A worried frown creased his brow. Angelina's theatrics had sucked him in. Over her niece's head, Talia caught his eye. She winked and mouthed the words, *"drama queen."*

The furrows in his brow deepened. Talia shook her head. Her niece had the man in the palm of her chubby little hand. "Let's go see what's left of the buffet Sophie and Aggie set out."

The calamity was cleared up, and the evening passed in a merry haze of food and fun. After everyone ate their fill of oyster stew, spicy meat pies, and macaroni and cheese, pictures were taken in front of the tree. Only then were the children allowed to open the small boxes that had tempted them all afternoon. Each box contained a Christmas stocking hand sewn by Sophie. When the fire died, the men helped the children hang them from mantle hooks.

It was late when the children set out cookies and a glass of milk for Santa. Hanna and Angelina dumped reindeer food into a metal bowl and placed it next to Santa's goodies.

Talia brushed a few wayward oats off the stone hearth into her hand. Holding them, she remembered her first day at SeaMount. The girls were mixing the magical oats. That day her life had changed. Memories cascaded one after the other through her mind's eye. With trembling hands, she dumped the oats into the bowl.

Ethan's fingers brushed her nape. She glanced up, into his questioning face, and smiled tentatively. "Please push me to the piano." She had to release the whirlwind of emotion the memories stirred within her, or she would burst wide open.

Her fingertips stroked the smooth ivory. She executed several fast runs followed by a lively Christmas song. The music drew everyone in, and soon they were singing and sharing in the joy spilling from her heart and across the keyboard. With each song, the tempest inside her grew calmer. She ended the sing-along with a soothing rendition of "Silent Night."

After the last note died out, Gray took Hanna from Sophie and quietly announced it was bedtime for his girls.

Talia pushed away from the keyboard. If Santa was to make his appearance, then Angelina and Simao needed to be off to bed as well. Ethan placed Angelina on Talia's lap for a ride up to the suite.

Contentment filled Talia's heart as she helped her niece change into her jammies. Together, they recited the bedtime prayer Talia had learned as a child. Angelina was asleep before the "amen" was said.

At the door of Simao's bedroom Talia listened to Ethan pray and wish him a goodnight. She wiped the moisture from her lashes and tried to pull back before Ethan saw her, but she was too late. He pushed her into the living room.

"You're tired." Sitting on the edge of the sofa, he pulled her chair around so she faced him.

"Yes, but it's a good tired."

His gaze drifted over her face. "You should have been in bed hours ago."

"I wouldn't have missed this evening for anything."

A shadow passed over his face. "I'm thankful you *didn't* miss it."

"Me, too." She wasn't sure who moved first. He pulled her close and claimed her lips with a kiss that was filled with promises. Promises she longed to hear as she snuggled in the shelter of his arms.

A soft knock on the door broke them apart. "Come in."

Sophie entered and paused, her eyes going from one to the other. "I thought I'd help Talia prepare for bed, but I can come back…."

"No. Now is fine." Ethan rose. He stroked Talia's hair and gave her another heartfelt kiss. "You're sure about tomorrow morning?"

She squeezed his hand. "I'll meet you downstairs in the morning just like we discussed earlier." Exquisite shivers ran up her arm as he brushed his warm lips across the back of her hand.

"Sleep well, Tallie." He left the room, closing the door softly behind him.

Sophie looked contrite. "I'm sorry I interrupted."

Talia shook her head. "Thank you for coming. I'm exhausted." With Sophie's help, she changed into her silk pajamas and nestled between the bed sheets.

Saying goodnight, Sophie switched off lights as she left.

Drifting to sleep, Talia's bedtime prayer amounted to one sentence. "Thank you, Lord." He was all knowing. He'd understand what was in the depths of her heart.

Chapter 18

"Ouch." Ethan held up his hand to see if the wayward screwdriver had drawn blood. Bleeding all over Angelina's princess pedal car would not be cool.

"Should've let me do it." Whit knelt at the low coffee table, arranging furniture inside a three-story dollhouse.

"I'm almost finished." Ethan refused to admit defeat. He didn't remember having this much trouble when he put together toys for Josh. He paused, waiting for the familiar jab of pain that always accompanied thoughts of his son. But none came. He felt only the weight of the bone deep sadness that settled in after a great loss.

He stared unseeing at the pink car, uncertain how he felt about the pain fading away. Would he forget Josh? His heart hammered. *You can't forget. You won't forget.* He resisted the urge to run to his room to study the family photo while holding the little angel in his hand.

"Do you think we went overboard?" Logan rolled a blue and silver dirt bike into the room. Gabe followed carrying a pink tricycle. Streamers dangled from neon handgrips.

"Nah. Kids gotta have Christmas." Gray tied a bow on the last steel runner sled. Five of them in varying sizes stood on end along the railing. He and Sophie had chosen to spend the holiday with their SeaMount family. The girls were all for making Santa's job easier with one stop.

Caleb and Charlie entered the room carrying colorfully wrapped gifts. They added them to the pile that was creeping from beneath the tree and threatening to take over the room.

Sam limped in jingling car keys. "Guess Santa has already visited." He dropped the keys into the toe of Davie's stocking. His eyes traveled the length and breadth of the room. "How'd we come to this?"

"Kids in the house."

"And women."

A general murmur of agreement filled the room that was decorated to the hilt and near bursting with gifts.

Sam flashed a lopsided grin. A swipe of his pointed finger included Whit, Caleb, and the St. John brothers. "Heaven help us when the four of you find women."

"Not happening."

"Not in this life time."

"Gonna be a long wait."

"Never."

Amid the protests, Ethan exchanged a knowing look with Gray.

Christmas morning arrived early. Ethan stifled a yawn as he waited at the elevator for Talia and the children to make their appearance. He hadn't liked her show of independence last night, but he understood it. He glanced into the sitting room. Beyond the glowing tree, Whit and Caleb argued over how much reindeer food to trail out onto the porch to look real.

Ethan shook his head. Santa's cookies had disappeared in a flash last night. Waiting for morning to disperse the oats had been a unanimous decision. The men hoped the wind off the ocean wouldn't blow the grain away before the children saw "evidence" that Santa's reindeer had enjoyed the magical food.

The elevator door slid open, and a rambunctious crowd spilled out. Gray's girls led, followed by Angelina and Simao.

Sophie hurried after them. Over her shoulder she called out, "Merry Christmas."

Gray rolled Talia's wheelchair off the elevator. "Here she is."

Ethan's breath caught in his throat. Talia was dressed in a dark green lounge set. He swooped in for a good morning kiss. "Merry Christmas."

"Merry Christmas." Her eyes sparkled, and her smile showed no lingering strain from the accident.

"How are you feeling this morning?"

"A little sore…and so happy to be here." Her gentle smile sent his heart into a flip.

Squeals of excitement cut the moment short. Ethan pushed her into the sitting room.

She gasped. "Who are all these gifts from?"

"Santa."

She squeezed his hand. "You're spoiling them."

Ethan grinned wide. "Have a heart, woman. Every man here is guilty of overdoing. You have no idea what this means to us. We've all missed Christmas at home more times than we care to remember." He caressed her cheek. "Today is a celebration." He couldn't resist kissing the soft smile on her lips. "You'll receive your gift later when we're alone."

The pandemonium soon settled to a dull roar. Dressed in tulle princess gowns, Angelina and Hanna played with the dollhouse. Lissa's new tablet held her enthralled while Andi played with a kid's CSI field kit. The men followed Davie to the lower parking lot to inspect the new-to-him sedan that belonged to the keys in his stocking.

Ethan helped Simao adjust the seat on his new bike. "Want to take it for a spin?"

Simao whooped, and Talia clapped her hands over her ears.

"Com'on then. Too slushy outdoors, but the hall is long enough for a slow ride."

Sophie stepped behind Talia's chair. "While the men and children play, let's help Aggie and Ava with breakfast."

The day passed in a joy-filled blur ending with an exhausted Simao and Angelina asleep in their beds.

Finally, Ethan had Talia to himself.

His heart beat hard in his chest as he helped her into her coat, hat, and mittens. In another week school would be back in session. He had to act now or she'd return to her life in the city, and she'd take the children with her. He wheeled her into the elevator.

"Where are we going?"

"Up." The night on the beach, he'd held back telling her one thing. The time had come to share it with her.

The elevator stopped. He pushed her chair through a small, dimly lit foyer and out onto a private deck. A strong wind blew off the ocean. White foam trimmed the waves thundering ashore. He'd finagled to get the Christmas lights on the building switched off. Overhead, stars twinkled like gems against the black sky.

"Put your arms around my neck."

Bracelets tinkling, she linked her hands at the back of his coat collar.

He lifted her then sat in a wide deck chair settling her on his lap. Talia rested her head in the hollow of his shoulder. For a few minutes they sat quietly, enjoying the night air and each other's company.

Unable to wait any longer, he reached into his pocket and pulled out a small velvet box. He held it out to her.

Lips pursed in a silent, "*oh*," she hesitated. For a long moment she studied his face. "Ethan, are you—?"

"Just open it. Then we talk."

She lifted the lid. "Oh, Ethan." Gold music note earrings were cradled in white satin. The head of each eighth note was set with a large oval cut diamond. Five dainty diamonds were set in each flag. "They are beautiful."

Her breathy whisper caused his pulse to trip. He wasn't about to let any opportunity to kiss her get past him. Her arms crept around his neck as he pressed gentle kisses to her lips, cheeks, brow, and the tip of her cold nose. Her husky chuckle sent fire coursing through his veins.

She pulled back. "My gift for you is in the basket of the wheelchair."

Reaching over, he snagged the handles of a canvas boat bag. Its weight surprised him. He helped her lift out a box wrapped in silver paper and tied with a blue bow. A look of uncertainty hovered in her eyes, intriguing him.

"I hope you like what I got you." She shoved the tote to the floor and rested the box on her lap.

Prepared to love it, no matter what it was, he untied the bow and peeled off the paper to reveal a blue box. She helped him lift the lid.

He pushed aside the folded tissue paper that protected a picture frame. Afraid the low light was playing tricks on his vision, he paused. Realizing what was in the frame set his heart thumping hard in his chest. Hands shaking, he removed the silver frame from the cushioning paper. "You named a star…for Josh." Tears blurred the coordinates and registry number until they merged with the certificate's swirling cosmic background. Unable to speak, he ran his fingers across the protective glass.

"There are two others in the box."

She helped him take them out. His late wife's name was printed on one. "My Angel" was printed on the other. "Ever see a grown man cry like a baby?" He pulled her close and buried his face in the curve of her neck.

"I guess you like them?" Her mittened hand smoothed across his shoulders.

He huffed a chuckle into her hair. "They are perfect." He breathed in the mandarin orange scent she wore. *You are perfect.* He took a deep breath. "Do you remember what Simao asked Santa for?"

Her eyes roamed over his face before she answered, "He wants you for a father."

Peace settled over Ethan. "I'd be proud to be his father."

Her voice trembled. "Simao and Angelina—can't replace Josh and Angel."

She had it all wrong. He shook his head. "I couldn't place that burden on them. God is *adding* to the blessings in my life." He ran his hand down the sleeve of her coat. "I don't expect them to step in as substitutes. No more than I'd expect you to replace Lacey."

She jolted straight up. Her eyebrows dove to meet over the bridge of her nose.

Before she could speak, he huffed a frosty breath and propped his brow against hers. "Before we met, I saw you, too."

"In your dreams?" Her voice shook.

"No. My eyes were wide open. First time that ever happened."

"God gave you a vision of me?" Talia clung to him, her world spinning. He hadn't told her this the night of the open house.

He wrapped his arms around her. "I was surprised, too. At the time, I was sure I'd never again give away my heart. But I can't imagine a future without you, Tallie. You and the children." His kiss was warm and sure. "I love you."

His whispered words sent a low vibrato fluttering through her. She relaxed into his embrace. This man loved her. He loved the children. They loved him. Her heartstrings twanged with recognition. *She loved him.*

"Will you marry me, Tallie?"

She buried her face in the neck of his jacket. Engulfed in his masculine scent, she pressed close to the pulse beating strong and steady beneath her cheek.

His fingers were warm on her jaw. "Your answer better be 'yes.'" His lips replaced his fingers, nibbling the sensitive spot beneath her ear.

She giggled. "You're tickling." *Wrong thing to say.*

He targeted her neck with a noisy lip-smacking vengeance.

His warm breath and bristly cheek melted her into a weak puddle of shivers and giggles. Blinded by happy tears, she tried to push him away. His knit cap slipped off.

He lifted his head. "I have to warn you, I'm highly trained in methods of interrogation. It would be best to give me the answer I want to hear."

Talia couldn't keep her hands to herself. Yanking off her mittens, she tossed them over his shoulder. She smoothed her hands across his temples and traced the curve of his ears. "I suppose Santa would lose some of his magic if he failed to deliver Simao's wish." She blinked hard and tried to look serious.

His eyes sparkled with a devilish glint.

Leaning her brow against his, she stared into his eyes. Like a bow on violin strings, his heated gaze drew from deep inside her beautiful yearnings for a life with this man at her side.

"I have no idea how or when it happened, but my heart and soul are yours, Ethan Thomas." She took a deep breath. "That thrills me, and scares me, and isn't at all what I planned for my life." She snorted indelicately. "I didn't plan on discovering I had a sister, or a nephew and niece, either."

"God has a way of surprising us."

"Does He ever." Tightening her arms around his neck, she pressed her lips to his for a warm, thrilling moment before drawing away. Her words came out in a breathless rush. "I love you, Ethan, and yes, I'll marry you."

"Whoooo hoooo!"

"Oooooh!" Talia's world spun as her exuberant, brand new fiancé twirled around. She held on, marveling over his strength. Running a possessive hand across the width of his shoulder, she relaxed in his arms. "How far do you plan on carrying me?"

"Look up. To the most distant star and back again."

She smiled. "That's awfully far."

"I plan on it taking forever." His lips claimed hers, and her heart tumbled softly. Long moments later, lightheaded from love and lack of oxygen, she pushed at him breaking off the kiss.

He frowned. "We need to work on your lung capacity."

She gasped for air.

"You gonna pass out on me?"

"No."

"Good. We aren't done yet." He carried her around the curve of the deck, passing several curtained windows before stopping at a door. "My hands are full. Please turn the doorknob."

Talia craned her neck to see where he was taking her.

He twisted sideways to go through the doorway and into the warmth of a softly lit room. A sparsely furnished great room included a kitchen to the left and a living area to the right.

"Who lives here?"

He set her on the tall stool at the kitchen counter. "No one, yet."

Yet. Her heart banged hard in her chest, stealing the breath she'd only just gotten back.

Chapter 19

Ethan started with the top button of her coat and undid them slowly one by one. He slid it off her arms setting her bracelets to jingling. Next, he unwrapped her scarf from around her neck and placed it on the granite counter with her coat and hat. "If you like this apartment, it's ours."

"Ours?"

"Sam has several residences in this wing." He carried her down the hall. "Three bedrooms—enough room for our family, Tallie. And when I'm away, I'll know you and the children are safe here."

She sighed dramatically. "You're going to be overprotective, aren't you?"

He growled. "Absolutely." He turned a full circle in the empty master suite. "Get used to it." They ended up where they began. Still holding her, he settled on a kitchen stool.

"Like the place?"

"I love it. There's so much to consider. So much to do. I have Papa and my career."

"We'll figure it out together. Charlie is gathering information on the Alzheimer units here in town. You can take your pick."

"School for the kids?"

"Public or private. Your choice."

She glanced up at him. “My career? I love teaching, Ethan.” A troubled note thrummed through her words.

He frowned. “I won’t lie. I prefer you not be exposed to danger like you were that day we met.” He kissed her brow. “God has given you a beautiful gift, Tallie. I will never ask you to stop sharing it. But perhaps how you use your gift will be different here. All we can do is trust that God will show you where He wants you. He brought us together. He has a plan.” Ethan kissed the tip of her nose and sent a quick prayer winging heavenward before asking the next question. “How long do you need to put together a wedding?”

She lifted her head. “A woman dreams about her wedding. All that planning takes time, you know.” Her lips quivered, and she pressed them together.

The tease. He was more than ready to call her bluff. “And a man dreams about his wedding night. All tha-*mmmph.*” Her warm hand covered his mouth. He’d forever remember her wide eyes and shocked squeak.

When she was sure he wasn’t going to continue, she removed her hand.

He wasted no time indulging in playful kisses as retribution. She’d stopped him from speaking, so he’d just have to make his point in a much more tangible way. He nibbled his way around her ear, down her cheek and across her chin, reveling in her laughter. But in the course of doling out justice, he found himself on the receiving end of his own payback. His heart broke open, and restitution poured in. He claimed her lips, deepening the kiss as the need to be made whole spiraled thorough him.

Her fist banged against his chest.

He raised his head leaving her gasping like a beached fish. “I really do need to teach you some breathing techniques.”

"Won't help... Ethan Thomas.... You'll always take my breath away."

His heart tumbled deeper in love than he'd been only moments before. He brushed his lips lightly across hers. "Even with a lot of practice?"

She sighed and leaned into him. "Even with a lifetime of practice."

Epilogue

Valentine's Day

Talia peeked into the gaily-decorated common room. Nurses and aides helped their elderly charges find seats. Mr. Finnegan, the school dean, and several of her New York friends sat together chatting.

Her father looked handsome dressed in a tux. He sat at the front of the room with two young men. One sat at a piano and the other on the throne of a drum set. They were students from the Manhattan School of Music here to play improv around Papa's six notes. As wedding marches went, hers would be unique, but giving Papa his last real gig filled Talia with unspeakable joy.

She faced the floor mirror set up especially for the occasion in the manager's office. Turning her head from side to side, the music note earrings Ethan had given her winked with brilliant sparkles.

"You look lovely." Sophie straightened the short sweep train of Talia's white floor length sheath.

"Thank you for being my matron of honor." Sophie looked stunning in a red, one-shouldered gown. Talia hugged her close. "And thank you for helping me plan my wedding on such short notice." Her own sister had been lost to her, but God in His goodness had provided *this* woman to be the sister of her heart.

Angelina skipped across the room clutching a hair wreath. She spun in a circle making the bell skirt of her red dress flare. "Help me, Mommy."

Mommy. Sweet joy swept through Talia. She used the wreath's attached comb to secure the circle of baby's breath in her niece's curls. "There you go, sweetie." She double-checked the clasp on the pearl necklace she'd given Angelina as a wedding gift.

Someone tapped on the door.

"Yes?"

Caleb, the self-appointed wedding director, stuck his head inside. "Ready?"

She nodded, and he opened the door a little wider.

"I'll go." Kissing Talia's cheek, Sophie slipped out as Simao entered.

He wore a red rose on the lapel of his tux. The air around him hummed with barely contained excitement.

"My, how handsome you are, Simao."

He peeled back the sleeve of his tux. An onyx cuff link glinted in the French cuff of his shirt. "Dad helped me with these."

When Ethan and Talia announced their engagement, the children had started calling them Mom and Dad. Their desire to be a family was all consuming. Waiting on a wedding, or the formal adoption papers mired in the legal system, did not make sense to Simao and Angelina.

A heavy-handed knock followed a scuffle outside the door.

"You can't go in there." Caleb's voice left no room for negotiation.

"Hold onto your boutonniere. I'm *not* going in."

Ethan. Talia whisked the train of her gown out of the way and hurried to the door. With a finger to her lips to quiet the children, she pressed her ear to the crack between door and casing.

"Just want to pray with her before the ceremony."

"Everyone is seated. We have to do this now before Mr. Kroger decides to visit the head for the third time. Like herding cats out there."

Talia clapped a hand over her mouth to muffle her giggle. Her bracelets chimed giving away her presence.

"Tallie?"

"Fine." Resigned, Caleb relented. "But hurry up, and no peeking at the bride."

"Tallie." Ethan's voice drifted through the crack.

Positioning herself behind the door, she opened it a tiny bit. "Yes?"

The tips of his fingers reached through. "Take my hand."

She opened the door a smidge wider and let him squeeze his entire hand inside the room. Holding it, she motioned for the children to come closer. She positioned their hands on top of her and Ethan's. Warmth radiated up her arm and cascaded through her. The rush of blood in her veins made hearing all of Ethan's whispered prayer impossible, but the phrases she caught burrowed deep within her heart to be cherished for all the years to come.

They were a family starting a new life together. Why had she questioned this? Her heart cried out, thankful for a God who knew her better than she knew herself. Belatedly, she chimed in with Simao and Angelina and said, "Amen."

She let go of Ethan's hand and kissed the children. "What do you say? Time for Mommy and Daddy to become husband and wife?"

From the other side of the door she heard several masculine snickers.

She bumped the door shut with her hip. How many of the men were out there listening to her and Ethan's moment? *Get used to it, Talia. You'll be living the married life in a fishbowl.* A grin played across her lips. Truthfully, she couldn't wait to become a member of the SeaMount family.

She smiled at the children. "Are we ready, darlings?"

"Yes." They were barely able to contain their excitement.

Taking up her bridal bouquet of red roses and white calla lilies, Talia turned to Simao. "Tell Uncle Caleb, we're coming out."

Ethan stood beneath an arch of tissue paper flowers and glittery hearts created in craft class by the elderly women now giggling and pointing like schoolgirls. Residents of the facility, friends of Talia's, and the men from SeaMount filled the room. Her minister was there to officiate.

He was proud of her. Including her father in the ceremony meant more to her than a picture perfect wedding in church. She was beautiful inside and out. This time tomorrow, her father would have a room in a new facility in Rhode Island, only a few miles from the SeaMount Agency's headquarters. She could visit him daily. Ethan was happy he could give her that gift.

At Caleb's signal, the drummer picked up his sticks and set the rhythm. Talia's father took the cue and played his repetitive notes. The pianist joined in, and a beautiful melody filled the room.

The manager's office door opened, and Ethan's heart lurched hard. *His family.* Love filled him to overflowing. He pulled out his handkerchief and wiped his eyes. After such a dark time of loss, God had surprised and blessed him beyond anything he'd ever imagined possible.

Beautiful in a dress that hugged her curves, Talia walked toward him with Simao and Angelina on either side. All three glowed with happiness.

Angelina ran the last few steps and leapt into his arms. He hugged her and passed her to Gray, his best man. Simao took his place between the two men.

Sophie took the bride's bouquet.

Ethan took Talia's hands. Her bracelets chimed sweetly.

Like a thousand stars, love shimmered in her eyes leaving him with the unfamiliar feeling of breathlessness. Her radiance dispelled the last of the shadows he'd carried too long in his heart. From this day forward, he would live in the light of her love.

THE END

Thank you for spending time reading Ethan and Talia's story. I hope you have found encouragement for your own faith journey. If you enjoyed this story be sure and tell your friends. If you have a moment, would you please leave a short review on the site where you purchased *Under Starry Skies*? It doesn't have to be long. Even two or three words would be wonderful. Reviews are not only the highest compliment you can pay an author, they also help other readers make informed choices about purchasing books and discovering new authors. Thank you so much! God bless.

Anita

P.S. If you would like to know about new releases and sales, please sign up for my newsletter!

http://eepurl.com/A1Wkz

Also by Anita Greene

OUT OF THE WILDERNESS
INTO THE DEEP

Learn more about Anita
or sign up for her newsletter at her website:

anitakgreene.wordpress.com

About The Author

Anita lives in Rhode Island with her husband, son, and spoiled Belgian Malinois. When she isn't writing, she enjoys reading, gardening, needlework, sewing, and making cards. She hopes to one day get all her photos into scrapbooks.

Made in the USA
Columbia, SC
11 July 2018